12.7.18

D1584017

HOOFBEATS WEST

When Jess Caird, owner of the White Sage, finds one of his cowhands murdered and a barn set on fire, he sets out with old-timer Horner to bring the culprit to justice. Evidence points to Caleb Grote, a notorious gunslinger, and the trail leads to the settlement of Sand Ridge. There, Caird encounters businessman Dugmore, head of the local Pony Express which employs Caird's nephew. Is there a connection between Dugmore and Grote . . . ?

Books by Colin Bainbridge
in the Linford Western Library:

COLIN BAINBRIDGE

HOOFBEATS WEST

Complete and Unabridged

LINFORD
Leicester

First published in Great Britain in 2015 by
Robert Hale Limited
London

First Linford Edition
published 2017
by arrangement with
Robert Hale
an imprint of
The Crowood Press
Wiltshire

A catalogue record for this book is available
from the British Library.

ISBN 978–1–4448–3304–1

Published by
F. A. Thorpe (Publishing)
Anstey, Leicestershire

Set by Words & Graphics Ltd.
Anstey, Leicestershire
Printed and bound in Great Britain by
T. J. International Ltd., Padstow, Cornwall

This book is printed on acid-free paper

1

Jess Caird stood on the veranda of the ranch house, lounging against the doorframe. The heat was oppressive and the air shimmered. Flies buzzed and droned and he swatted them away with his Stetson. He looked across the burned, arid landscape towards the distant hills, his eyes screwed against the blazing sunshine, searching for the missing rider, but there was no sign of him. He had sent him out as far as the hills to look for strays and it shouldn't have taken too long to roust out any that still kept to the coulees. Even so, he wouldn't have worried too much except that there had been trouble recently. Two hired hands had been beaten up during an altercation in town and another wounded in a shooting incident. That was within the last month. Turning on his heel, he began to make his way towards the corral at the rear of the building. The horses stood with their heads drooped, except for the roan gelding which was all saddled up. Old Horner was holding it by the reins and stroking its nose while he talked to it. He looked up at Caird's approach.

'No sign yet?' he said.

Caird shook his head. Horner stroked his stubbled chin. 'Guess it's beginnin' to look bad.'

'Yup, especially in view of what else has been happenin' lately.'

'You mean....' The horse tossed it head and Horner stroked its nose to calm it, not finishing his sentence.

'There's no one better with those horses,' Caird commented. 'You sure got a way with 'em.'

'I don't know about that, but I appreciate you takin' me on,' Horner replied. 'If anythin' went wrong, I don't know what else I'd do. I ain't much use to anyone any more.'

'Guess we're both gettin' a bit long in the tooth,' Caird responded. His eyes lifted towards the distance. 'I'm gettin' restless waitin' around here,' he said. 'I reckon I might take a ride up to those hills and see if I can find anythin'.'

'I figured you might do that,' Horner said. 'That's why I got Trojan here all ready for you.'

Caird grinned. 'You can read me like a book,' he said.

'Want me to string along?' the oldster asked.

'Nope. You wait here and keep a lookout in case Philips finally turns up.'

Caird was about to step into leather when he turned and made his way back to the ranch house instead. In a few moments he reappeared carrying a rifle.

'You're taking that old Paterson along?' Horner remarked.

'Yeah.'

'You think you're gonna need it?'

'I don't know. But it pays to be prepared.'

Horner watched as Caird slid the rifle into its scabbard. 'Be careful,' he admonished. Caird turned back to face the oldster.

'Don't worry. I won't be takin' any chances,' he replied, as he hoisted himself aboard the big roan.

'Sure you don't want me along?' Horner asked.

'You stay here. He might turn up yet. I'll be back before sundown.' Without waiting for a reply, Caird touched his spurs to the horse's flanks and set off in the direction of the hills.

The distance between the ranch house and the high ground was deceptive and it took him longer than he anticipated reaching the foothills. Raising himself in the stirrups, he glanced across the shimmering landscape. The White Sage buildings lay like a child's cast-off toys. There was no sign of Horner. After a few moments he rode on again. The air was cooler when he entered the pass and the contrast was striking. He rode more slowly now, letting the horse pick its own way while he looked about him. The passage widened and he was almost through to the other side when he saw buzzards hovering and knew what to expect.

The cowhand's body lay stretched out just off the trail and, at a little distance his horse, a pinto, stood with its head hanging, chomping the grass. There was no sign of any cattle. Coming up to the body, Caird dismounted and, taking his rifle, approached carefully. It lay front down and two gaping bullet holes between the shoulder blades told their own story. Kneeling down, he gently turned the body over. It was Philips. The face that stared up at him seemed somehow younger than he recalled. He cursed under his breath and then looked about him. There were plenty of places that the killer could have concealed himself — behind a rock or a patch of vegetation — but taking into account the probable trajectory of the bullet, he picked out a couple of spots that seemed the likeliest and began to make his way towards them. He was right first time and it was easy to work out what had happened. Judging by the traces which had been left, he figured there had been only one attacker and he had come in from a side trail leading further up into the hills. Once he had worked things out to his satisfaction, he made his way to where the horse was standing. It looked up nervously at his approach and began to back away, but he soon had it under control. Puzzled, he looked all about him. What was he to make of it? His thoughts were interrupted by a sudden flash of light from higher up the hillside. He glanced in that direction but could see nothing. It was probably only sunlight glancing from a rock but on the other hand it could be glinting from the metal of a gun barrel. For a moment he considered riding on up to investigate, but then thought better of it. There was no point in taking the risk. Instead, he took the reins and led the horse back to where the body lay. After a considerable effort, he succeeded in hoisting it on to the animal's back, and then remounted his own horse. Leading the pinto with its sad cargo, he set off to retrace his steps to the ranch house, occasionally glancing behind him to check that no one was following.

The day was far spent and shadows of night were beginning to fall by the time he got back. Horner was waiting as he rode into the yard with an anxious expression on his face.

'You found him then?' he said, when he saw the body dangling across the pinto's back.

'Yeah. Help me get him down.'

Together they lowered the body of the youngster and laid him on the packed earth of the yard.

'Ain't no point in delayin' it,' Caird remarked. 'Best put him straight in the ground.'

'What about the rest of the boys?'

'They'll know soon enough.'

It took longer than expected to dig a grave deep enough and by the time they had finished it was late. The sky was clear and filled with stars and an orange moon hung low on the horizon. When they had cleaned themselves up Horner produced a bottle of whiskey and they sat outside at a rickety table. Neither of them had spoken much but after they had taken a few swallows they began to talk.

'What do you make of it?' Horner asked.

'I don't know. We've had some trouble lately, but now it's got serious.'

'You figure it might have something to do with those offers you've had for the White Sage?'

Caird grunted. 'Offers!' he repeated. 'I don't know who's behind 'em, but whoever he is, he must be jokin'.' He took a swig of whiskey. 'We ain't had any trouble in all the time I've been ranchin' here till now. I might have put those other incidents down to chance, but this is somethin' else.'

'Yeah. This is more than a coincidence.'

'It's downright bloody murder and I aim to do somethin' about it.'

The oldster scratched behind his ear as his eyes swivelled towards the hills. 'Whoever did it, he ain't far away.'

Caird produced his tobacco pouch and, after rolling a quirly, handed it to the oldster. When they had lit up, Caird suddenly shook his head.

'We can't just take this lyin' down,' he said. 'Whatever's goin' on, we'd be out of business pretty damn quick if we did. But that ain't what's upsettin' me: what gets me is thinkin' about that young fella we just laid in the ground. He was no more than a boy. And we're responsible for what happened. We took him on. We gave him the job.'

'Nobody could have anticipated this.'

'I'm the owner of the White Sage. The responsibility lies with me.'

'You ain't plannin' on windin' things up? I know things have been hard and we're short of men, but you wouldn't sell the old place?'

Caird thought for just a moment. 'Of course not,' he said. 'I got to admit there have been times in the past when I've thought of doin' just that, but this just makes me more determined than ever to keep the place goin'.'

'Well, it looks to me like somebody is sure tryin' to get you to quit.'

'Yeah,' Caird said, 'looks that way to me too. But who could it be? The White

Sage is only a small enterprise after all. None of us is likely to make a fortune.'

Horner looked behind him at the ranch house. It was in need of repair, like the corral from which the soft breathing of the horses just reached their ears. 'Sorry about that last remark,' he said. Caird gave him a puzzled look. 'I mean, for thinkin' even for one moment that you might consider windin' things up. That ain't your style, or mine either. We both know what we've got to do.'

Caird leaned forward and slapped the oldster on the shoulder. 'You're damned right,' he said. 'We're gonna deal with this, startin' tomorrow when we take another ride up into those hills. Nobody and nothin' is gonna run us out.' He glanced toward a rough wooden board which marked the grave of the youngster they had just buried. 'More than anythin' else,' he said, 'we owe it to him.'

Silence fell between them. The moon rose higher and from somewhere in the distance they heard the faint howl of a coyote. When the bottle was finished they rose to their feet and made their way inside.

It was not long before dawn when Caird awoke. For a few minutes he lay still, listening carefully. He could hear nothing except Horner's troubled breathing coming from an adjoining room. He reached for his six-gun and, taking care not to make any noise himself, he eased the bedclothes aside. He stood up and made his way to the partly open door. A faint light illumined the main room beyond and he watched closely for any sign of movement. Once he was sure that no one was there, he made his way through to Horner's room and glanced inside. The oldster lay on top of his mattress, still fully clothed. He turned and made his way back through the main room before easing the door ajar and stepping out into the night. Again he stopped to listen closely, but the night was still. Then why were his senses warning him that something was not quite right?

Suddenly one of the horses in the

corral snickered and he began to walk in the direction of the sound, keeping to the shadows. He reached the back of the building and took time to observe the scene before him, bathed as it was in the translucent light of the moon and stars. The horses seemed a little restless, but there was nothing to suggest they had been disturbed by anything other than a sense of his own presence. A little way to the right of the corral was a run-down barn and he was about to make his way in its direction when his nostrils picked up a faint acrid smell. His immediate reaction was that someone nearby had rolled a cigarette when he saw the first thin roils of smoke begin to curl from the side of the building. They grew denser and then he finally realized that the building itself was on fire. He ran forward, reached the doorway and threw himself inside. Already flames were beginning to lick the walls and they were rapidly mounting higher; the crackle they made was like the hissing of a hundred snakes. He ran to the water trough, filled a bucket with water and hastened back. He threw the water on the flames but it was totally ineffective. The dry wooden walls of the barn were just so much tinder to the fire. He ran towards the ranch house and began to call out at the top of his voice:

'Fire! Fire!'

Men began to emerge from the bunkhouse, confused and dishevelled, but it didn't take them long to realize what was happening as they moved towards the blazing barn.

'Do what you can!' Caird ordered. 'Try and prevent it spreading!'

The building was well ablaze now and the first tongues of flame began to appear from the roof. The heat was growing more intense. Suddenly a figure staggered out of the doorway, his clothes on fire. It was Horner. He stood for a moment, irresolute, till Caird, ignoring the flames, dragged him to the water trough and half threw, half dragged him into it. The flames were instantly doused and after a moment Horner's head appeared above the surface of the water, spluttering and coughing.

'Are you OK?' Caird said.

The oldster looked at him confusedly before coming to his senses. 'I think so!' he said. 'I guess I was stupid to go inside. Lucky you were around.' He rose up, the water running from him, and with Caird's assistance climbed awkwardly over the rim of the water trough.

'This damn leg,' he muttered.

'Hell, I reckon that's the first bath you've had in years,' Caird commented.

The oldster grinned, but before he could reply a loud crash rent the air and a section of barn wall collapsed in a huge shower of sparks.

'Get back!' Caird yelled. 'There's nothing we can do to save it now.'

Suddenly Caird had a thought and started to run towards the ranch house. He dashed through the open door and looked all around before continuing up the stairs. By the time he came back down Horner had appeared.

'Thank goodness!' Caird ejaculated. 'I thought for a moment they might have started somethin' here too.'

' 'They'?' Horner repeated.

Caird looked at him with a steely glint in his eye. 'You don't suppose this was an accident either?' he said. Without waiting for a reply, he turned on his heel and set off for the scene of the fire. Somebody had loosed the horses and two of them ran past him, their frightened eyes glinting in the lurid light of the flames. He turned to watch them and caught sight of Horner struggling along behind him. The sight of the oldster made him pause and he looked at him closely when he came alongside. Steam was rising from his clothes and he had a singed look about him.

'Are you sure you ain't hurt?' Caird asked. 'Those flames sure seemed to have caught hold.'

'I figure you got me to the water in the nick of time,' Horner replied.

The roar of the fire grew louder as they approached the burning building, which was creaking and groaning like a live thing. As they watched, another wall came toppling down. The heat was intense and it wouldn't take long before the entire structure collapsed. The men had taken Caird's advice and stepped back. They watched in a kind of fascinated horror as the fire leaped higher, illuminating the night and filling the air with showers of sparks. Finally, with a kind of shudder, the barn collapsed in on itself.

'That's it,' Caird said. 'There's nothin' to be done till mornin'.' At his words, the men began to wander away till only Caird and Horner remained.

'I guess whoever started the fire must have got out pretty quick,' Caird remarked. 'I might have scared him off myself.'

Horner, a miserable figure, continued to stare at the blackened barn. 'So what do we do now?' he asked finally.

Caird shook his head. He wasn't looking forward to the morning. The destruction wrought by the fire was nothing in comparison with what he had to tell the hands about the murder of Philips. Horner looked up at him. His features were grim and a nerve was twitching in the side of his jaw.

'Like I said, whoever did this can't be too far away,' he remarked.

Caird seemed to consider his words. In the flickering glow of the dying flames he looked almost unnatural. 'How are your trackin' skills?' he asked.

'Not so good, but maybe good enough,' the oldster replied.

'I reckon Drysdale can look after this place till we're ready for the trail drive,' Caird said.

'Yeah. Drysdale's a good foreman. He knows the ropes.'

'Once we've settled things here,' Caird resumed, 'we'll head for those hills and take a closer look at where I found Philips. We might be able to pick up the sign of whoever shot him.'

For a few moments more they stood beside the smoking ruins of the barn, and then turned away and began to walk back to the ranch house.

Despite feeling an urge to be on the trail,

it took some time for Caird to gather the men and make his explanations. He had to arrange for the organization of the ranch while he was away, and it was quite late in the day by the time he and Horner finally made their departure and rode away towards the hills.

'Maybe we should have taken a couple of the men along with us,' Horner said. 'Some of them really wanted to come.'

'I thought about it,' Caird said, 'but I figure this is a job for just you and me. None of 'em signed up to anything like this. Besides, they'll be needed to keep a lookout on the White Sage. I have a feelin' whoever started that fire won't be back in a hurry, but the boys will be sure to be extra careful from now on.'

They rode steadily, climbing to the foothills and the limits of the White Sage range till they reached the spot where Caird had discovered the body, where they dismounted.

'This is right where you found him?' Horner queried.

'Yeah. See those rocks over there? I

figured that's where the killer was hidin' and sure enough it's where I found those shell cases.'

'Did you ride on any further?'

'Nope. I rounded up the loose horse and headed back to the ranch.'

'Let's take a look up there,' Horner said.

Leading their horses, they walked the rest of the way. Horner was limping slightly and Caird gave him another look.

'Are you sure you didn't get hurt back there?' he said.

'I'll be fine.'

They had almost reached the rocky outcrop and Horner was looking closely at the ground. He stepped aside a little way and then called out to Caird.

'Over here. Horse droppings.'

Caird joined him. The droppings were easy to see and before long the oldster's keen eyes picked out traces of horses' hoofs.

'I ain't any kind of tracker,' he said, 'but I'd take a guess there were at least three horsemen. The way I see it, the rest waited up here while the person who did the actual shootin' rode on down and took up his position.'

Caird nodded but didn't say anything. He was thinking hard. The killing seemed to have been organized. Even if the victim had been a random choice, it was a purposeful act.

'You may not be an expert,' he said to Horner, 'but do you figure you could follow that sign?'

Horner looked up with a grin. 'I figure we could make a real good try of it between us,' he said.

Caird thought for a moment. 'Let's make a start. We didn't get any sleep last night so we'll see how we go. We've got some supplies but we could do with pickin' up more.'

'Ain't there an old tradin' store somewhere off in that general direction?' Horner said, nodding towards the crest of the slope down which the three riders appeared to have come.

'There used to be. I don't know if it's still there. But if it is, there's a chance those varmints stopped by on their way here. We might get lucky and pick up some more information.'

Without further comment, they made their way back to the horses, climbed into leather, and set off once more, following the sign. It was slow going. Neither of them was skilled in the art of tracking and every so often they had to stop and dismount to take a closer look. The ride took them over the top of the hill to a long plateau and then down again into another valley. Despite being in high country, the sun was hot and beat down unrelentingly. Eventually they found a narrow arroyo with a trickle of water running through, shaded by a few drooping cottonwood trees, and decided to call a halt. They were both feeling exhausted after all the exertions of the previous night and the subsequent ride and, although he made light of it, Horner was feeling the effects of the fire. His clothes had protected him, but he had still suffered minor burns to his arms. He had inhaled a good deal of smoke and his lungs and chest felt tight. He fell rather than dismounted from his horse.

'Rest up,' Caird said. 'I'll see to everything.'

While Horner stretched out, Caird made up a fire, filled the kettle with water from the stream and made coffee. After handing a tin cup of the steaming black liquid to Horner, he looked in his saddle-bags for some strips of jerky.

'Sorry, but this is gonna have to do until we can get those supplies,' he said.

'You got some tobacco?'

'Sure have.' He reached in a pocket for his pouch of Bull Durham and handed it to the oldster. Then, as an afterthought, he pulled out a battered silver flask.

'Try addin' some of this to your coffee,' he said.

Horner poured some of the whiskey into his cup and took a swig. 'That sure feels better,' he said.

Caird did the same and then they sat in silence for a time while they made the best of their meagre repast. The oldster stretched out his leg.

'That old injury botherin' you?' Caird

asked.

'It hurts some, but I'm used to it now. Must be some kinda poison in a cougar's bite.' Caird threw him an inquisitive glance. 'That's the way it happened,' Horner said. 'Jumped me and had its teeth in my flesh before I had time to do anythin'. Lucky for me my pardner had the wits to scare it off with a brand from the fire.'

'When did that happen?'

'A long time ago. We were pannin' for gold but we never found anythin'. Leastways, not enough.' He paused for a few moments, musing. 'Funny thing,' he continued, 'but I've heard of fellas keeping cougars as a pet.'

'Never heard that before,' Caird replied.

'No reason why you should.'

As evening drew on, the air grew cooler and Caird was about to throw some branches on the fire when Horner held his arm.

'What is it?' Caird asked.

'It just occurred to me. Whoever those

23

varmints are set fire to the barn, they can't be too far off. It might not be to wise to give away our position.'

Caird gave Horner's comments a moment's thought. 'You've got a point,' he said, 'but there's another way of lookin' at it.'

'Yeah, what's that?'

'Well, it could save us a lot of time and effort if they did pay us a call; so long as we're ready for them.'

The oldster grinned. 'Yeah, I see what you mean.'

Caird tossed the branches on to the fire. 'It's gettin' dark,' he said. 'If they're somewheres about, they'll soon be able see this for miles.'

The oldster's grin spread wider. 'Yeah. Let's make it a real warm welcome if they do decide to drop in.'

Caird got out his sack of Bull Durham again and rolled another smoke. He passed the sack to the oldster, who did likewise. They were quiet for a while, enjoying the tobacco, until Horner spoke again.

'Supposin' those varmints don't stop by, how long do you reckon to take tryin' to track 'em down?'

'That's a good point. We set off after them just as quick as we could, but I don't know how long we'll be able to keep on their trail. We're findin' it hard enough already to follow their sign. If it was down to me, I'd just as soon keep on goin', but there are other things to think about.'

'That's what I was meanin'. We've pretty well completed roundin' up those cattle critters and they'll soon need to be on the hoof. By the way, didn't you mention somethin' about your nephew, Evan, joinin' us for the drive? Shouldn't you be around if he turns up at the White Sage?'

'That ain't a problem any more. Last I heard from his mother, he's apparently changed his mind about the idea. Seems like he's come up with another scheme and has decided to apply for a job as a rider with that new pony express they're plannin' to set up. I don't know too much about it, but it sounds like a hare-brained sort of venture to me.'

'What's he want to do that for?'

Caird shrugged. 'I guess he's old enough to make his own decisions and face the consequences. He can look after himself. I was thinkin' more about the whole shebang. Anyway, the prospect of Evan showin' up at the White Sage is one less thing I need to worry about.'

'How old is the young whippersnapper now?'

'Nineteen, goin' on twenty. I haven't seen him or his mother in a whiles, but I'm told he's turnin' out good. A mite restless maybe, a bit wild, but I guess there's nothin' wrong in that. Havin' his old man Jock Buchanan run off not long after he was born probably didn't help a lot. He's still tryin' his hand at different things, I guess. I expect he'll settle soon enough.'

Horner laughed. 'Hell, look at how we were at his age; he's got plenty of time.'

His words seemed to induce a wistful silence. An evening breeze had sprung up and rattled the leaves of the cottonwoods. The firelight flickered and danced as it blew cross the clearing. Outside the circle of their fire, darkness had settled over the land like a cloak. Caird drew deeply on his cigarette and then flicked the stub into the flames. He glanced at Horner. Despite himself, the oldster seemed to have succumbed to tiredness and the lulling effect of the warmth. His eyes had closed and his chin was resting on his chest. Caird smiled and, rising softly so as not to disturb him, moved silently to his horse and drew the Paterson from its scabbard. Selecting a spot at a little distance away the fire, from which he had a good perspective over the surrounding country, he made himself as comfortable as he could to watch and wait. Despite what he had said to Horner earlier, he wasn't expecting any trouble. The gunmen, whoever they were, would be some distance ahead. He was more concerned with the question of how he and Horner might catch up with them and what they would do if they succeeded.

2

The settlement of Sand Ridge wilted in the heat. It owed its existence to two things: the stage station and the river landing. It still didn't amount to much, but the owner of the stage line, a man called Dugmore, had big plans for developing it further, mainly by establishing the new pony express mail delivery service. He already owned many of the main public buildings and businesses, including the real estate office, the livery stables, blacksmith shop, and the Eastwater Hotel and Saloon. It was at the latter that he sat at table with a couple of other men, smoking a cigar and enjoying a glass of Madeira.

'Well, gentlemen,' he said, stretching out his legs under the table, 'I've set out the details of the proposed enterprise and I think you'll agree it's a sound investment. In fact, it's a lot more than that: it's an opportunity for you to get in on the ground floor of something that's going to put the name of Sand Ridge firmly on the map.'

'I ain't so sure,' one of the other men said. 'A thousand miles is one hell of a long way. Are you sure you can cover the distance in five days?'

'Take another look at the map, Hobley. It's all there. Relay stations every fifteen miles apart. The riders will travel at full gallop and switch ponies at every station.'

'How far can one man cover?'

'Seventy-five miles. Altogether, two hundred miles a day. Easy.'

Hobley whistled. 'It still sounds like a tall order to me.'

'Of course it isn't simple, it'll take a lot of organizing. But it can be done.'

'How much time do you need?'

'I'm ready to go right now.'

The other man raised his head with a look of enquiry on his smooth features. 'It's gonna cost plenty,' he said. 'I just ain't so sure.'

'You're not usually so coy about

makin' a stack of money,' Dugmore replied. 'Believe me, Trimble, it's a solid investment.'

'I guess you've got a government contract lined up?'

'I've been talkin' it over with Senator Robertson,' Dugmore replied. 'It's taken care of.'

Trimble took a sip of the Madeira. 'There's one other thing bothers me,' he said.

'Yeah? And what might that be?'

'Didn't you mention previously that there's some kind of issue affecting the matter? Something about a ranch lying right across the route you propose to take? Seems to me that might complicate matters some.'

'It isn't a problem. In fact, I'm dealing with the issue right now. You could say I've just about reached an agreement with the proprietor. In any case, it doesn't stop me goin' ahead. It just means that for the moment I have to take a more circuitous route.'

'You're operatin' on a tight budget,

don't that mean extra costs?'

'Like I say, it's a very temporary situation.'

'The proprietor — he's willin' to sell?'

'The way things stand, he ain't got much choice in the matter.'

Trimble and Hobley exchanged glances. 'What do you say?' Hobley asked. 'Do we go ahead?'

'Have I ever let you boys down before?' Dugmore interjected.

Trimble looked at him closely. 'This scheme seems a little more reckless than some of the others,' he said.

Dugmore tossed back the last of his wine. 'Look,' he said, 'it doesn't bother me if you want to miss out on the chance of makin' a fortune. There are plenty of other people who would be interested. If you wish to back out, I'll go it alone if necessary.'

Hobley put out a hand and touched Dugmore's arm. 'Hold it right there,' he said. 'Of course we're with you on this. Ain't we, Trimble?'

Trimble hesitated for a moment before

a smile spread across his features. 'Of course,' he concurred. 'Just makin' sure, that's all.'

Dugmore nodded and then reached out to the bottle of wine to refill their glasses. 'Gentlemen,' he said, 'I give you the Dugmore and Company Overland Mail Express.'

When they had finished, Dugmore got up from the table. As far as he was concerned, business was concluded and he had no desire to spend any more time with his two companions than he had to.

'I'll be in contact very soon,' he said.

They rose and, slightly unsteadily, made their way out of the dining room. Dugmore stood for a few moments and then sat down again. He drew another cigar from his pocket, bit off the end and lit it. Presently the door to the room opened and the waitress appeared. As she made her way to his table, he eyed her approvingly.

'Will you be wanting anything else, Mr Dugmore?' she said.

He looked her up and down. 'Now that

just depends on what you're offerin',' he said.

'I mean, would you like to order anything else?'

'You're new here, aren't you?' Dugmore said.

'Yes, this is only my second day.'

'What's your name?'

'Miranda, but people call me Mandy.'

'Well Mandy, why don't you sit down here beside me and have a glass of wine.'

'I couldn't do that. I'm not supposed — '

'Just one glass. That's all I'm suggesting. Seems a pity to let it go to waste, don't you think?'

She made to move away but he reached out to stop her. 'Are you new in town?' he asked. 'I don't think I've seen you before.'

She didn't reply and pulled her arm away from his grasp. Dugmore suddenly laughed.

'Do you know who I am?' he said.

'No.'

'I'm Leroy Dugmore and I own this hotel.'

He looked her up and down, waiting

for a response, but she only looked confused and uncertain what to do next. Dugmore continued to laugh but it was suddenly cut short.

'Do you like your job?' he said. She nodded. 'Then I'll give you some advice: if you don't want to lose it, you'd better make sure you give the customers what they want.'

There was still no response.

'Go on,' Dugmore said finally. 'You can go now, but I expect we'll be seeing each other again.'

Without saying anything, she turned and made her way back to the kitchen. Dugmore watched her approvingly, then took a few more pulls at his cigar before placing it, largely untouched, into an ashtray. He got to his feet and made his way out of the dining room, through the foyer and out into the heat of the day. He stood for a moment, taking in the scene, and then began to walk purposely towards a narrow plank bridge which crossed a creek-bed at the end of the main street, shaded by a grove of cottonwood and willow trees. Just beyond it was another part of town, a run-down section that the decent citizens tended to avoid, which ended at the landing and the river. Passing a couple of deserted shacks and a barber shop, he came to a low straggling building across the front of which was scrawled the one word: *Logan's*. Giving the place a look of disdain, he passed through the batwing doors.

Inside the place was heavy with smoke and a stale smell comprised of sweat and sawdust. There was a pool table and several card tables and at the back, a long plank which served as a bar. Gathered around it was a group of men who straightened up at Dugmore's approach. One of them stepped forward and, with an awkward gesture, removed his hat.

'Howdy, Mr Dugmore,' he said.

Dugmore did not reply and the man fidgeted before glancing at the barman as if for assistance.

'Would you like a drink, Mr Dugmore?' the barman said.

'No.' He turned to the other man. 'Is

Grote back yet?' he asked.

'I don't think so.' The man turned to a couple of the others beside him. 'Has anyone seen Grote?' There was no response and he turned apologetically back to Dugmore.

'No one's seen him,' he said.

Dugmore gave him a hard stare. 'When he gets here,' he said, 'tell him to report to me and pronto.'

'Sure, Mr Dugmore. I'll tell him right away.'

Dugmore turned on his heel and made his way back through the fumes. When he had got as far as the batwings, he turned back. The place was silent and the men at the bar were watching with anxious and drawn faces.

'Grote should have been back by now,' Dugmore commented. 'I'd hate to think that he might have let me down.' Without waiting for a reply, he turned and pushed his way outside. He stood for a moment, breathing the dusty air, before beginning to make his way back towards the main part of town.

Caird awoke with a start. He realized he must have fallen asleep and for a few moments his head felt heavy and confused, but he knew that something had disturbed him. He glanced behind. Horner lay curled up wrapped in his blanket by the ashes of the fire. He reached for his rifle but it wasn't there. He was about to get to his feet when he felt the prod of a six-gun in his back and a low voice said: 'Don't try anythin'. Just turn around real slow.'

Caird did as he was bid. The man facing him with the revolver in his hand was about the same age as himself but was dressed in an odd garb of faded buckskins. He wore moccasins on his feet.

'What is this?' Caird said.

'I was about to ask you the same thing.'

'Why don't you put that shooter away and we can talk like sensible people.' The man seemed to weigh up his words for a moment, and then to Caird's surprise, he lowered the gun and slid it into a belt tied around his waist.

'I wasn't expectin' that,' Caird said.

'I figure I can weigh a man up. You don't look to me like the sort who would cause trouble.'

'Why would you think we might be?' Caird asked.

'I got reasons.'

Before either of them could say anything further, there was a noise from Horner's direction as the oldster shuffled in his blanket. Caird glanced at the sky.

'Can't be long till dawn,' he said. 'Why don't I get that fire goin' and you can join us for a spot of breakfast?'

'I could sure use some coffee,' the man said.

In a few moments Caird had woken up Horner and apprised him of the situation. The oldster looked at the stranger but didn't make any comment. Caird soon had the fire blazing; he placed some bacon in the skillet.

'Need a hand?' the newcomer said.

'Nope. But you got me kinda puzzled about who you are and what you're doin' here.'

'Sorry about the way I went about introducin' myself,' the man said. 'The name's Kitson, Slade Kitson. I got me a cabin further back in the hills.'

When Caird and Horner had introduced themselves, Kitson said he would go and get his horse which he had picketed at a little distance.

'Do you trust that *hombre*?' Horner asked.

'I think so. After all, he had the drop on me. Sorry about that, by the way. I must have fallen asleep. I could have got us both killed.'

As he turned the bacon, the stranger returned leading a wiry paint. 'That bacon sure smells good,' he remarked.

'It'll be ready soon. Take a seat, make yourself comfortable.'

Neither Caird nor Horner were in a hurry to question the stranger, although they were both curious as to who he was and what he was doing there. But to ask a lot of questions too soon wasn't the way they went about things. Presently the breakfast was ready and nobody said much as they ate, other than a comment from Kitson that it was very good.

'Good coffee too,' Horner replied.

When they had finished, Kitson put his hand in a pocket of his buckskin jacket and produced a pouch of tobacco and some cigarette papers, which he passed round. Only when they had lit up did Caird think to question the stranger, but it was Kitson himself who spoke first.

'I guess you must be wonderin' what I'm doin' creepin' up on you like that in the middle of the night.'

'I was kinda curious,' Horner remarked.

'It's like this,' Kitson said. 'As I said, I got me a little cabin in the hills. It ain't much, but it suits me fine. I don't hold with company and I don't get many visitors. I can live easily off the land and what supplies I need I can get at the old trading station at Rowan's Bottom.'

'That must be the place I had in mind,' Caird interposed, speaking to Horner.

'It's not used much now,' Kitson said.

'Rowan can't make any kind of profit out of it. He's an old man now. That didn't stop him from taking a beating though. I was down there recently and I found the old chap in quite a bad way. Naturally, I did what I could for him. He told me a group of riders had come by and taken stuff. When he tried to argue with them, that's what they did.'

Caird and Horner were suddenly very interested. 'Three riders, you say?' Caird said.

By way of reply Kitson gave him a questioning look tinged with suspicion. 'You know somethin' about those varmints?' he asked.

'Maybe,' Caird responded. In as few words as possible, he outlined what had happened to the White Sage. 'Could be the same three,' he concluded.

'Funny thing is,' Kitson resumed, 'I think I've seen them before. One night I'd just turned in when I heard hoofbeats. Like I say, my place is kinda remote so it seemed odd for anyone to be up there, and even more odd that they would be ridin' by night. I got up, grabbed my rifle, and went outside. The hoofbeats got louder and then I caught a glimpse of them. They were still some distance away but it was a clear night and I got good eyesight. There were definitely three of 'em. I figured I might be in for some trouble, but they rode on by. Probably they didn't even see my cabin — it's set back in a grove of trees.'

'That still don't explain what they were up to.'

'Me and Rowan go back a'ways. We were both mountain men in the old days. I didn't like what had happened to him. I figured I might try and find the lowdown coyotes who did it. I traced 'em out this way and when I saw your firelight, I figured it might be them.'

He paused for a moment and they took a moment to reflect on what had been said. Caird drew out his own tobacco pouch and handed it round and they refilled their tin cups.

'There's one more thing,' Kitson eventually resumed.

'Yeah? What's that?'

'Rowan gave me a name. One man seemed to be in charge and the other two let it drop when they were speakin'. It was Grote.'

Caird and Horner thought for a moment. 'Not Caleb Grote?' Horner remarked. 'It couldn't be him, could it?'

'I see the name means something to you,' Kitson said. 'I don't exactly get around much, but it registers with me too.'

'Caleb Grote,' Caird reiterated. 'One of the most notorious gunslingin' killers west of the Mississippi. And mean as a weasel. I came across him once myself. If it's the same man.'

'We ain't got any proof of that,' Horner said.

'Maybe not, but beatin' up a defence-less old man would be right up his street,' Caird replied.

Horner stroked his chin. 'Maybe you're right,' he said, 'but it still doesn't explain why Grote would have suddenly turned up in these parts. As far as I know, he hasn't been seen or heard of for some time. So what would he be doin' here and now?'

'I don't know,' Kitson replied, 'but I'll tell you another funny thing. As I said, my cabin is pretty remote and I don't get many visitors, but just recently I've noticed strangers passin' through. One time I saw a couple of people with some kind of instrument down in one of the valleys. I couldn't figure what they were up to, but they were up to somethin'.'

'You think it might be connected with Grote and his *compadres*?'

'I couldn't say, but for sure it's a coincidence.'

Horner had been listening carefully while Kitson was talking. 'Those people you saw,' he said, when there was a pause in the conversation, 'you don't suppose they could have been measurin'?'

Kitson turned to him. 'Measurin'?' he repeated. 'Why, yes, I guess that just about describes what they were doin'.'

'What are you thinkin'?' Caird asked.

'I'm thinkin' that maybe they were

surveyors.' Horner turned to Caird. 'What was that you were sayin' about your nephew?' he asked.

'My nephew? What's he got to do with it?'

'Weren't you tellin' me he's tryin' to get a job with some new overland mail company? Well, maybe that's what they were measurin' — layin' out a route for the Pony Express.'

The others exchanged glances. 'Could be he's right,' Kitson said.

'That still doesn't explain what Grote was doin' in these parts.'

The remark served to silence them. Daylight had come as they were talking and without adding anything further, Caird got to his feet and began to douse the fire.

'I don't know about you two,' he said, 'but I figure I've done enough thinkin' for now. I reckon we'd best be hittin' the trail.'

It didn't take long to remove all traces of the camp and they were soon ready to mount up. Caird and Horner exchanged glances over the pommels of their saddles.

'I don't know what you got in mind to do now,' Caird said to Kitson, 'but you're welcome to string along with us.'

'I was hopin' you'd say that,' Kitson replied.

'It makes sense. We're all after the same thing.'

'Mind if we swing by Rowan's Bottom? I'd like to check on the old man, see if he's OK?'

'Unless the trail leads in some other direction, it suits us,' Caird replied. 'We could do with pickin' up some supplies.' He took a last glance over the scene of their campsite and then swung into leather.

'OK,' he said, 'let's ride.'

Evan Buchanan sat in his room in the Eastwater Hotel contemplating the situation in which he found himself. He had come West with the intention of working on his uncle's ranch, the White Sage, and assisting with the cattle drive. Instead, if things went as he hoped, he was about to take up a position with the Dugmore and Company Overland Mail Express. He had acted on something of a whim. One of the first things that had drawn his attention when he arrived in town was a large notice on which was written:

New! Pony Express: Riders Wanted. Are you young and looking for Adventure? $50 a month and board.

He had to report to a place out of town which went by the name of Saddletree Station. Glancing at his reflection in the mirror, he jammed his Stetson on his tangled mop of hair, buckled a gunbelt around his waist, and went clattering down the hotel stairs, slamming the door behind him.

He reached the bottom and was about to enter the lobby when his progress came to a sudden halt. Just emerging from the dining room was the most beautiful girl he thought he had ever seen. She was carrying a tray with a bottle and some glasses on it and she was coming straight

47

towards him. He had a vague impression of strawberry-blonde hair tied up in a bun and a pair of blue eyes, but he was in no situation to take anything in very clearly. As she approached him she smiled, and, for a moment they were slightly entangled as she sought to pass him. He smelt her perfume and managed an awkward smile back as he belatedly raised his hat. She acknowledged the gesture with a barely perceptible nod and then she was past him. He turned to look at her departing figure but, feeling it wasn't the thing to do, quickly turned and made his way outside. He stood for a moment, thinking about her. Who was she? It didn't take much reflection to realize she must be an employee of the hotel. In that case, an opportunity might arise to speak to her, to find out more about her. Feeling considerably agitated at the prospect, he turned and made his way to the livery where his horse was stabled.

He had asked the whereabouts of Saddletree Station and been informed that it was a disused relay station on the old stage route which had recently been refurbished. He had ridden for some time in the direction indicated and was looking out for any of the landmarks when he saw a couple of riders approaching. He brought his horse to a halt as they came alongside. One glance told him he was in trouble.

'You'd best turn right around, sonny,' one of them said. 'This here is private property and Mr Dugmore don't like trespassers.'

'I guess I must have taken a wrong turning.'

'I ain't interested in reasons. Just do like I say.'

'I'm lookin' for the Saddletree Station. Do you know it?'

Buchanan had sized the men up; they looked like gunslingers. They regarded him closely and then suddenly one of them whipped out his pistol.

'I'm gettin' kinda tired of tellin' you to leave,' he said. 'I figure I'm goin' to have to teach you the hard way.'

'I ain't lookin' for trouble.'

'Well, it sure as hell looks like you found it.'

'I'm leavin' right now,' Buchanan said, and made as if to turn his horse. In a moment, however, he had his Colt in his hand and before anyone could react, he had pulled the trigger. The bullet smashed into the man's hand, sending his pistol flying in the air. The gunman gasped in pain as his companion's horse reared, almost sending its rider crashing to the ground.

'Like I said, I wasn't lookin' for trouble, but I'm ready to meet it if it comes along. Now I suggest you all turn about and start ridin'.'

'You won't get away with this,' the second gunnie said. 'From now on you'd better watch your back.'

'Yeah, I guess that's the way your sort operates. Now, get movin' before I'm the one to lose patience.' For a moment the two men seemed to hesitate before one of them spoke.

'Better get you to a doc, Wheeler,' he remarked. With the injured man still wincing in pain, they finally turned their horses and began to ride back in the direction they had come from. Buchanan watched them till they were out of sight and then rode away.

It didn't take him long to realize where he had gone wrong. He had been advised to follow a fork in the trail, and he had simply taken the wrong one. When he had travelled a little way down the new track, he knew he was heading in the right direction by the things he had been told to watch out for. The last one was a narrow passage through some rocky outcrops on either side of the trail, and when he reached the summit of some rising ground, he saw the relay station ahead. It was built of logs with a corral and shelter stalls for the ponies. Even from a distance he could tell that the horses were in good condition — mustangs carefully selected, he guessed, for toughness and speed. It would be good to ride one of them.

He rode up, dismounted, and tied his horse to a hitch-rail. The door to the cabin was open and he peered inside. It was gloomy, but he could see a man sitting at a table who looked up at his arrival.

'Come on in!' he called. Buchanan shuffled inside. 'Well, boy, what can I do for you?'

'I want a job, ridin' the mail.'

'You don't beat about the bush,' the man commented. He looked Buchanan over and then guffawed. 'Hell, come back in a few years,' he said.

'I want that job now, not in a few years.'

'You ain't old enough or tough enough.'

'I'm nineteen years old, nearly twenty. And I reckon I'm tougher than I look.'

The man laughed again. 'Maybe you're right,' he said. 'Tell me, what's your name?'

'Evan Buchanan.'

'You reckon you can ride?'

'Anythin' you can cinch a saddle on.'

The man thought for a moment before getting to his feet. 'Come with me,' he said. Buchanan followed him out of the room.

'That your horse?' the man said, nodding towards the sorrel.

'Yeah.'

'Grab the saddle and bring it along with you.' Buchanan did as the man said and then they made their way to the corral.

'OK,' the man said. 'Let me see you saddle up one of those mustangs and ride him.'

Buchanan eyed the horses closely. There were six of them in the corral and he chose one, big and well muscled. It looked back with a gleam in its eye and its ears were cocked. Buchanan could see that it was nervous. Hefting the saddle, he opened the gate and walked into the corral. As he neared his chosen horse, it began to back away and he attempted to reassure it with some softly spoken words of encouragement.

'Steady, old fella,' he said. 'Easy.'

As he talked, he approached it from an angle till he was able to stroke its forehead. Gently but deftly he slung the saddle over its back and commenced to tie the cinches. The mustang shuffled forward as he took hold of the saddle horn and climbed into the leather. He didn't know what to expect. Clearly the man he had spoken to anticipated some sort of reaction from the mustang; at the very least the horses were probably spirited and fresh. The mustang had accepted the saddle, but he had no idea how well they were saddle-broke. As his feet found the stirrups, the mustang began to move its neck and toss its head, stepping sideways, but a tug on the reins brought it straight again.

'Good boy,' he repeated. 'How about you and me go for a ride?'

The horse's head went down and for a moment Buchanan feared it might jump, but after a few worrying moments he had it under control as it settled to a steady walk. He rode it out of the corral and then, touching his spurs to its flanks, he encouraged it to open out. As the horse stretched forwards, Buchanan could sense the power in its flanks and the fire in its chest. The mustang gathered speed and as the wind began to blow past Buchanan's face, he couldn't resist breaking into a holloa of sheer exhilaration. It was only after some time that he thought of the man back at the relay station and brought the horse to a halt.

'I reckon you and me are goin' to hit it off,' he said, stroking its mane. It was with reluctance that he turned it round.

When he arrived back at the relay station, the man was still standing where he had left him by the corral. 'How long have I been gone?' he asked.

'Long enough for me to see you can ride that there animal.'

'He's quite a horse.'

'Yeah. He's got plenty of spirit. A horse is no good without spirit.'

Buchanan dismounted and removed his saddle. 'Well,' he said, 'do I get the job?'

The man grinned. 'Sure. Come with me back to the office and we'll make it official.'

When Buchanan had taken the mustang back to its place in the corral, the two of them made their way to the main building, where the man pulled a few crumpled papers from a drawer.

'I take it you can sign your name?' he said.

Buchanan didn't reply but wrote his signature. When he had finished the man put the papers back in the drawer and then produced from within it a bottle of whiskey and a couple of glasses.

'I'm not sure you're old enough for this,' he said, 'but I guess there's cause for some celebration.' He poured the whiskey and they both took a swig.

'I never did catch your name,' Buchanan said.

'Shefflin,' he replied, 'Lew Shefflin.'

'Pleased to make your acquaintance.'

When he had finished the whiskey, Buchanan was about to take his leave when Shefflin stopped him. 'There's one more thing I got to do,' he said. He reached into another drawer and this time produced a little leather-bound book and another sheet of paper on which was some writing.

'Here,' he said. 'Everyone gets to have a Bible and everybody signs the pledge.'

Buchanan ran his eyes down the sheet of paper. When he got as far as *I will refrain from drinking intoxicating liquors* his glance fell on Shefflin.

'You haven't signed anythin' yet,' he said, 'and it applies to riders, not to station keepers and stock tenders like me.'

Buchanan grinned, nodded and read on. *I will not get into quarrels or fights ... I will conduct myself appropriately at all times ... I will faithfully carry out the duties and tasks assigned to me ... so help me God.*

'It's somethin' to live up to,' Buchanan said. Shefflin handed him the pen.

'Yeah. Seems like bein' able to handle a horse and puttin' your life on the line just ain't enough,' he replied.

Buchanan signed and then made for the door. As he stepped into leather Shefflin appeared in the doorframe.

'Don't forget this,' he said, waving the Bible. Buchanan reached down, took the book and placed it in his saddle-bags.

'I expect I'll be seein' you when you come ridin' through with the mail,'

Shefflin said. 'If you get to do this section of the run, that is.'

Buchanan nodded, touched his hand to his Stetson, and was about to ride away when Shefflin stopped him.

'There's somethin' else I nearly forgot,' he said. 'Report back here in three days' time to get your final instructions.'

'What time?'

Shefflin tugged at his chin. 'Around noon should do it,' he said, 'but it don't really matter. I'll be around.'

Buchanan nodded and then, applying his spurs, rode away. It was only when he had almost reached town that he re-called what the gunman had said about trespassing. He had mentioned the name Dugmore, and it was the Dugmore and Company Overland Mail Express he had signed up to. Was there a connection? And perhaps more to the point: what had Dugmore to do with the gunmen? Maybe it would pay to make a few enquiries in town.

3

Caird and his two companions took the direction that Kitson said would take them to the trading post and continued riding. Kitson was more skilful than either Caird or Horner in following a trail, but it wasn't very hard to do and it was increasingly obvious that the men they were tracking were heading towards the trading post too. Kitson was concerned but didn't mention it to either of the others. Eventually the terrain grew wilder and it seemed to Caird that Kitson must have taken a wrong turn. The path they were following seemed to be little more than a trail made by deer or wild horses, and then he remembered Kitson's background as a mountain man. They were taking a cut-off and this was confirmed when the trail dipped down and they saw the trading post in the middle of an open basin with a stream running through it.

The store itself was long and low, made of logs with a brick chimney. Drawing to a halt, they sat their horses in order to take in the scene. Presently Kitson spoke.

'I don't know what it is, but somethin's not right.'

'It's quiet, but I don't suppose there's anythin' unusual in that,' Horner commented.

Caird was looking hard. 'The glass in the windows is broken,' he said, 'and the yard is all churned up.'

'I don't like it,' Kitson replied. 'I should never have left the old man, but I didn't figure those varmints would be back. Let's get on down there, but be careful.'

As they approached, their eyes continued to search for anything untoward and, when they were close, they saw hoof marks in the dust of the yard. Outside the store they dismounted and tied their horses to the hitch rack. Drawing their guns, they approached the open door of the cabin and then rushed inside. The store had been ransacked. The shelves lay broken; cans and cartons littered the floor and broken glass crunched beneath their boots. A barrel lay on its side and what furniture there was had been smashed. Passing through the store, they entered a room at the back; a glance was sufficient to show the same tale of destruction.

'Looks like Grote and his boys finished off what they started,' Caird said.

'Yeah,' Kitson replied. 'But where is Rowan?'

They passed outside into the sunlight and began to make their way towards the stream. Flies had gathered in a cloud above its banks and they were still a little way off when they saw a body lying face down on the edge of the water. They scrambled down to pull it clear and turn it over.

'It's Rowan,' Kitson confirmed. He had been shot twice in the back. Horner turned to Caird.

'You got those shell casings in your pocket?' he said. 'If there's a match, we got even more proof it was Grote did this.'

'We don't need any proof,' Kitson muttered. 'We know damn well who did it.' He looked about, his expression grim. 'They didn't even bother about leavin' a trail. It's as clear as daylight where they crossed the stream and carried on ridin'.'

'There ain't much we can do for Rowan except give him a decent burial,' Caird said. 'But for damn sure we'll catch up with the varmints. We just got one more reason for bringin' them to justice.'

'They had no reason to do this,' Kitson said. 'They musta come back just for the hell of it.'

They stood in silence, each of them trying to contain the anger they felt. The situation was made the more painful by the fact that Grote and his gang could not have got there very much in advance of them. They were hot on his tracks; with any luck they might even have got there in time to prevent the killing. It was this thought that persuaded Caird that they couldn't afford to delay too long. Their best chance of catching up with Grote lay in moving on as quickly as possible.

'We'd best lay Rowan to rest,' he said, 'and then get right back on the trail.'

Buchanan came downstairs the morning following his interview hoping he might meet with the waitress he had brushed into on the stairs, but he was disappointed. When he had eaten he sat back and looked out the windows of the dining room to the street outside, and after a few moments found that he was looking for her.

'Hell,' he said to himself, 'I'm ridin' for the Pony Express now. I ain't got time for girls.'

He got to his feet and made his way outside, determined to make some inquiries concerning the name Dugmore. It didn't take any time or effort. Making his way to the barber shop and taking a seat in the chair, all he had to do was let the barber lead the conversation.

'New in town?' the man said.

'Yeah. Got me a job ridin' for the new Pony Express.'

'What? Leroy Dugmore's latest venture?'

'I guess so. It's called the Dugmore and Company Overland Mail Express. There can't be more than one.'

The man paused for a moment, the scissors in his hand. Glancing at the man's reflection in the mirror, Buchanan thought he saw an odd look on his face, but he couldn't tell what it expressed.

'If I was a few years younger,' he said vaguely, 'I might have thought about applyin' myself.'

He carried on with the job, and for a while the only sound was the clicking of the scissors. Buchanan was waiting to see if he would say anything further, but when nothing was forthcoming he decided there was no point in beating about the bush and asked outright.

'So who is this Leroy Dugmore?'

The barber put the scissors down. 'Shave?' he asked.

'Sure.' Buchanan sat back and the barber lathered his face and neck. He turned to strop the razor.

'You don't know Leroy Dugmore?' he resumed. Buchanan had the impression the topic was ended but the barber seemed quite happy to carry it on. 'I guess you must be new in town. He owns most of it as well as runnin' the biggest ranch around these parts. Where are you stayin? The Eastwater Hotel?'

'Yeah,' Buchanan replied.

'That's his. So are the general store, the harness shop and the real estate office. And that's only on the respectable side of town. This place ain't much, but at least it's still mine.'

'What's the name of his ranch?'

'The Bar U. I figure there's a message there somewhere.'

Buchanan thought back to his encounter with the riders. He must have strayed on to Bar U territory. If so, what the barber said certainly seemed to fit.

'You appear to have some reservations about Dugmore,' he said.

The man seemed to backtrack. 'Don't get me wrong,' he replied, 'Dugmore's done a lot for this town. Without him it probably wouldn't even exist. I ain't got nothin' against him.'

'All the same...'

'Let's just say a man with as many head of cattle as Dugmore has, is gonna need a lot of land to graze 'em.' He stopped talking and just at that moment the door of the barber shop opened and another customer came in. Buchanan would have liked to question him further, but he sensed that the man had said all he was going to say even without the intervention. He sat back while the barber finished scraping his neck.

When he emerged from the barber shop, he was uncertain what to do next, but remembering something the barber had said, he eventually began to bend his legs in the direction of the plank across the creek bed which divided the town. Written in rough letters on the wall of the last building before the creek were the words: *Doc Burrow MD*. As he approached it, the door swung open and a couple of men emerged. One of them had his hand wrapped in a bandage and even before he recognized their features he knew they were the men who had accosted him the day before. They stood for a moment in the doorway, talking to someone behind, and then they turned away and clattered across the bridge. Buchanan waited a moment, listening to the thud of their boots on the bridge, before following them. The bridge itself was exposed so he dropped down into the dry stream-bed and cautiously came up on the other side just in time to see them disappearing inside Logan's saloon. For a moment he contemplated following them inside, but before he could arrive at a decision there was a thunder of hoofs as a group of riders charged into view from the far end of the street. A pistol shot rang out and then another as they swung down in front of the saloon into which the two men had gone, yelling, shouting and swearing at the top of their voices. They charged inside and there was a further burst of shooting and a general cacophony of noise. When it had subsided a little Buchanan took the time to wander over to the hitch rack and take a look at their horses. They carried the Bar U brand. After his experience of the day before, he wasn't entirely surprised, but it still raised a few questions in his mind about some of the people with whom Dugmore appeared to be connected. But then, he thought, it wasn't really any of his business, till he remembered he was now in Dugmore's employ. As such, it seemed he was in some very dubious company.

Caleb Grote's reputation with a gun was well deserved. Twenty notches carved into the grips of his hardware told their own story; nobody was likely to question it or ask how his victims had died. As far as he was concerned, it was of no consequence. He had just added the latest one to mark the slaughter of the old man at the trading post, and he was anticipating adding more.

Kitson hadn't been the only one to observe Caird's camp-fire the night after the burning down of the barn. Grote had seen it too and quickly realized that it was probably somebody from the ranch.

That particular operation had not proved entirely successful. The object had been to burn the ranch house as well, but he and he companions had been disturbed in the process. He wasn't ready to let anything like that happen again. Once he had ascertained through his field-glasses who was following him, he set about laying his plans. He had considered setting an ambush at the trading post, but in the end had contented himself with killing the old man. He had pressed on hard subsequently to get well ahead and find a suitable spot for the dry-gulching, and he figured he had found it. An outcrop of rocks on rising ground overlooking the trail made it ideal. All he and his companions had to do now was wait till their trackers showed up. He sat back, beginning to enjoy the prospect of some further killing, when he became conscious of the piping voice of one of the others, a man with a face like a stoat by name of Winthrup.

'How long do you reckon they'll be?' he whined.

'How the hell would I know? Just relax. They'll be here soon enough.'

'Maybe we should leave it. Maybe we should get straight back to Mr Dugmore. We've been gone too long as it is.'

'What's the matter with you? Are you gettin' scared or somethin'?'

'No, I ain't scared. It's just that Mr Dugmore — '

Winthrup didn't finish the sentence because at that point he found himself staring into the muzzle of Grote's .45.

'I ain't got time for this,' Grote snapped. 'Either you shut your mouth or I blow your head off. Which is it to be?'

'Hey, take it easy, Caleb,' the other man intervened. 'Let's just all ease up some.'

Grote's face was contorted with rage; for a moment it seemed like he might carry out his threat, but then he succeeded in bringing his anger back under control. The grimace was replaced by a wolfish grin.

'Rickman's right,' he said. 'Guess we're all gettin' a mite jumpy.' He slid the gun back into its holster and reached for his tobacco pouch. When he had built himself a smoke, he passed it to the others. 'Help yourself,' he said.

He returned to his original position, his back against a rock, and inhaled deeply. The smoke seemed to smooth something inside him. In contrast to his outburst of rage, he now felt cold and detached. That's how it seemed to be with him; it was nearly always one or the other.

Time passed. After the little altercation, there was no further trouble. Each man sat in silence, thinking his own thoughts. On his part, Grote was pondering on the necessity of having the other two along at all. He could have managed the whole thing quite nicely on his own. It was Dugmore who had insisted on him taking them. It was the sort of assignment he liked — the opportunity to kill and add just a little to his evil reputation. He had only a dim idea of what it was all about. Obviously Dugmore wanted to apply pressure to the White Sage ranch. He wanted to scare the owner. It was something to do with the new Pony Express he was setting up. Grote didn't understand how that was supposed to work either, but it didn't concern him. It was enough for him to be able to exercise his deadly trade and make a good living out of it. He wasn't much interested in anything beyond that.

When he had smoked a few cigarettes he raised himself up and put his field-glasses to his eyes. Away in the distance he discerned a faint smudge against the sky.

'OK!' he called to the others. 'I think they're comin'!'

There was an answering shuffle of feet as Winthrup and Rickman adjusted their positions. Grote checked his weapons and then took another look through the glasses. Sure enough, the party of three riders appeared in view, riding at a steady pace towards them. He couldn't help grinning to himself. By the time they got within range, they would present an easy target. As they approached, he peered through the binoculars at their horses in an effort to make out their brands. He had guessed aright: two of them carried the White Sage symbol. Gathering a ball of phlegm in his mouth, he spat it out in an arc and glanced across at the others, one on either side of the trail. Rickman looked relaxed but Winthrup already had his rifle raised. He regarded him for a few moments before turning his attention back to the oncoming horsemen.

The riders came on, their horses' hoofs kicking up dust. Occasionally one or the other would glance about him but there was no indication that they suspected anything untoward. Grote raised his Sharps in readiness and saw the others do likewise. The riders were still just outside rifle range; he waited for the right moment to give the signal to open fire when suddenly, without his authorization, a shot rang out. He turned his head to see smoke issuing from Winthrup's rifle. Livid with fury, he turned back and squeezed the trigger of his own weapon but the three riders had already dismounted and were seeking the shelter of the brush.

There was nothing to do but to carry on the assault and for a few moments the air was rent by the din of gunfire and the scream of hot lead. Smoke hung heavy, obscuring the view, but the whine of bullets ricocheting among the rocks told Grote that he and his companions were under fire too. It didn't take him long to make a decision. Carrying out a bushwhacking from a position of safety was one thing: getting embroiled in a fight to the death was another. Without even bothering to signal to the others, he began to slither away among the rocks.

When he had got a certain distance on his belly, he got to his feet and broke into a run, keeping as low as possible. The sounds of battle faded and it was only when he was convinced that he was completely clear that he straightened up and slowed down, panting furiously as he did so. He soon reached the spot where the horses were tethered and paused to recover his breath. It was then that he realized the sound of gunfire had ceased. For a few minutes he stood with his hands clapped to his sides, deep in thought. What had happened back there? Were his two companions dead? There was a good chance of it and, if so, it might be to his advantage. He didn't owe them anything and, when all was said and done, it was Winthrup's fault that they had got caught up in a gunfight at all. If he hadn't been so jumpy and opened fire before the signal was given, they wouldn't have been put in a position of danger. Dugmore had taken him on and made it quite clear what he expected from him, but even so, from Dugmore's perspective, maybe he had gone a little far in killing the oldster at the trading post. It was hard trying to work things out, and it was made harder by the fact that the three riders might suddenly appear at any moment. Finally he arrived at a decision. He needed to mount up and get away, but it might be expedient to set the other horses loose.

Quickly, he began to untie them, and had almost completed the task when he heard the sound of footsteps and

Winthrup and Rickman themselves appeared. Rickman took one glance.

'What are you doin' with those horses?' he snapped.

Grote thought rapidly. 'I figured we might need to get away quick,' he said.

'You mean you were gonna sneak away and leave us right here.'

Grote had laid his rifle down, but his six-gun was in its holster. Before either Rickman or Winthrup had a chance to realize what was happening, his gun was in his hand and throwing lead as, ignoring the usual trigger action, he fanned the hammer with the palm of his hand. The movement tended to drag the gun off target, but his victims were standing at point-blank range and there was no chance that he might miss. Down they went, clutching at their bodies as blood spurted from their chests and stomachs. It was over in a flash. For just a moment they lay twitching and then they were still. Grote slid the gun back in its holster and bent down to make sure they were dead. Once satisfied of the fact, he made his way to the frightened horses and finished the job of untying them. With little encouragement, they went charging off while he held the reins of his own sorrel. He climbed into the saddle and, with a last glance back at the corpses of his former companions and a grin on his face, he wheeled away from the scene. They amounted to nothing other than two more notches for his gun.

Buchanan was sitting at a table in the Marietta Eating House enjoying a pot of coffee and biscuits when the door opened and the marshal entered. He took a quick look around the room before coming over to Buchanan's table.

'Mind if I join you?' he asked. Without waiting for a reply, he pulled out a chair and sat down. The proprietor, an ample woman of middle years after whom the eating house was named, appeared and he ordered a cup of coffee and some flap-jacks. When they came he poured a mug of the steaming black liquid and offered a flapjack to Buchanan.

'You're new in town, aren't you?' he said.

Buchanan glanced from the badge to the man's features. His face was lined and he wore a trimmed moustache.

'Yes,' he replied. He was happy to co-operate so added, 'I've got me a job ridin' for the Pony Express.'

The marshal seemed to consider that for a moment. 'Is that so?' he said. He took a swallow of the coffee and glanced out of the window before continuing, 'My name's Bedford, Joel Bedford. I know who you are.' He paused. Buchanan shifted in his chair. He was beginning to feel a little uncomfortable.

'Whenever a stranger in town goes around carryin' a gun strapped to his side, I make a point of makin' his acquaintance. Especially if I receive a complaint that he's made use of it.'

Buchanan looked him straight in the face. 'I think I know what you're referrin' to, but believe me it wasn't my fault.'

'Maybe you'd better tell me just what happened. And while you're tellin' it, you can say what you're doin' in town in the first place.'

Buchanan quickly outlined the incident with the gunnies. 'Like I say,' he concluded, 'I was on my way to see a man about the job. Before that I was plannin' to work on my uncle's ranch but when the opportunity to ride for the Pony Express came up, I changed my mind.'

When he had finished the marshal grunted. 'Well,' he said, 'that ain't quite the way I heard it, but you can relax. I'm not about to throw you in the slammer. Considerin' the injured party in question, I'm inclined to believe your account of the matter. By the way, what's the name of this ranch you were headed for?'

'It's called the White Sage. It's a few days' ride from here.'

The name meant nothing to Bedford, but Buchanan's prompt reply seemed to satisfy him. He glanced at the handle of Buchanan's .45.

'Maybe I should be confiscatin' that weapon, but it ain't my policy. Leastways, not just at the moment. But take this as a warnin'.'

Buchanan nodded. 'Sure,' he said. 'Don't worry. You won't get any trouble from me.'

The marshal finished his mug of coffee and poured another. He bit into the remaining flapjack. Just at that moment the door to the tea rooms opened again and the girl from the hotel came in. Buchanan felt a slight constriction of the throat as she sidled past.

'Hello, Miss Glover,' the marshal said, raising his hat.

She smiled and returned his greeting before sitting at a table in a corner of the room. The proprietor emerged again and the girl ordered something in a low voice which Buchanan strained to hear. When he looked up the marshal was regarding him in a quizzical fashion.

'A nice girl,' he commented. 'Works at the Eastwater Hotel.'

Buchanan made a poor effort to appear indifferent. 'Oh yes. I think I may have seen her. I'm stayin' there at present.'

'I know her folks. Her father retired

recently, but he used to run a local grocery store.'

Buchanan wasn't sure why the marshal was volunteering this information, but he took it as a kind of friendly warning. If so, it was somewhat premature. He had yet to figure out a way of making an approach to the lady. The marshal took a final swig of coffee and then got to his feet. 'Nice to make your acquaintance, Mr Buchanan,' he said. He strode to the door and as he placed his hand on the knob, he turned back for a moment.

'Be careful,' he said. 'I hear that Express ridin' can be a dangerous business.' With those cryptic words he opened the door and went out.

Buchanan's eyes followed him as he crossed the street and made his way towards the courthouse and jail. His back was to the girl, but he was acutely conscious of her. He considered turning round but seemed incapable of doing so. Finally he got to his feet and moved to the door. It was with a conscious effort that he turned his head to look in her direction.

She looked back and gave a slight nod. So she remembered him? He summoned a feeble smile in return and then left the tea room, closing the door gently behind him. His pulse was racing and he couldn't seem to think straight. In general, he wasn't pleased with himself. It seemed he had missed another opportunity of making contact with the young woman. What was the name the marshal had called her? Miss Glover? But what was her first name? Annoyed with himself and his juvenile behaviour, he crossed the street and made his way to the livery stable.

Jess Caird and his two companions lay in concealment till they were satisfied that the gunmen who had laid the ambush had fled the scene. Cautiously, they emerged from the shelter of the scrub.

'We've been gettin' careless,' Caird remarked. 'We should have been prepared for somethin' like that.'

Horner dusted himself down and examined his body as if checking to make sure that he was still in one piece. 'Beats me how we're all still alive,' he said. 'We were sittin' ducks.'

'You figure it was Grote and his pals?' Kitson said.

'Yeah.' He looked about and saw their horses off at a little distance. 'Let's round 'em up and then take a look among those rocks. But don't take any chances.'

Once they had collected their animals, it didn't take any time to discover the bodies of Winthrup and Rickman.

'When thieves fall out,' Kitson commented.

'What do you mean?' Horner asked.

'Ain't it obvious? I think you'll find neither of the varmints was shot by any of us. That leaves one other suspect.'

'Grote,' Caird added, and the old mountain man nodded. Horner moved away to examine the ground.

'They obviously left their horses here. Grote must have scattered them. I figure we can find 'em if you want to take the time.'

'Leave 'em,' Caird said. 'They'll find their own way or someone will come across 'em.'

'Some are ours,' Horner added, almost wistfully.

'They'll have to take their chances. Right now it's Grote we're concentratin' on.'

'What about these?' Kitson added, nodding towards the two corpses.

Caird thought hard. Grote wasn't far ahead of them. As a single rider, he had the advantage over them, but every moment they delayed increased his chances of getting clear. On the other hand, his sensibilities revolted at leaving the corpses to the coyotes and buzzards, despite the fact that they had been lucky to survive their murderous intentions. He had to make an effort to curb his enthusiasm for getting back on Grote's trail.

'I guess we stay long enough to bury 'em,' he said.

Horner looked at him and then spat on the ground. 'Hell,' he commented, 'this is gettin' to be a habit.'

'Just be thankful it ain't one of us we're buryin',' Caird replied.

When the task was done, they wasted no time in getting back in the saddle. At first it was comparatively easy to follow Grote's tracks, but after a time they found it increasingly difficult. The ground was bare and hard and a hoof left little imprint.

'A few years back,' Kitson said, 'I would have found this easy. I reckon I coulda trailed any critter goin'.'

'Yeah,' Horner replied, 'quite a few years back.'

Kitson turned and his face broke into a smile in reply to Horner's snaggle-toothed grin.

'You and me both,' he said.

Presently Caird held up his hand as a signal for them to halt. 'We need to think about this,' he said. 'We could carry on ridin', but we can't be sure we're headin' in the right direction. Let's face it; whatever else Grote may be, he ain't no fool. Apart from anythin' else, he's probably takin' steps to cover his tracks.'

'He could even be leadin' us into a trap,' Kitson said. 'He's got to have a base somewhere. Maybe there's some kind of outlaw roost and we're headin right for it.'

Caird tugged at his chin. 'What's the nearest town to where we are?'

'There's a settlement at Sand Ridge,' Horner replied, 'over on the Eastwater Creek.'

'Could be that's where he's headed,' Caird replied. 'I figure we should make our way there.'

'Makes sense to me,' Kitson responded after a moment's consideration. 'Apart from anythin' else, the varmint is gonna need supplies.'

'Yeah, and so are we. If Grote operates in the area, as seems to be the case, we might pick up some gossip at the very least.'

'It's better than ridin' blind,' Horner said, 'and it seems like that's what we're doin' right now.'

Caird looked around him. The sun was low in the sky and shadows were creeping across the land. 'I reckon we've come far enough for one day,' he said. 'Let's make camp and then tomorrow we'll set our course for Sand Ridge.'

4

Dugmore was sitting staring out of the window of the luxuriously appointed living room of his Bar U ranch house when he spotted a group of three riders in the distance. As they got nearer he recognized the central one as Grote, but the other two were not Winthrup and Rickman as he would have expected, but two of his ranch hands.

'About time,' he mumbled to himself.

Grote had taken somewhat longer over his current assignment and since it closely affected his plans for the Pony Express route, he wasn't best pleased. He watched as the horsemen rode into the yard and dismounted. In a few moments there was a knock at the door.

'Come in,' he shouted. The door opened to admit his foreman.

'Grote is here,' he said.

'Thanks, Johnson. Take him over to the

bunkhouse. Let him clean some of that trail dust off his hide and then bring him back.' While his instructions were being carried out, he poured himself a drink and lit a cigar; by the time he had finished both, Johnson appeared with Grote in tow. Dugmore didn't waste time beating about the bush.

'Well,' he said, 'did you do what I told you?'

'Yeah. I figure those White Sage varmints won't be holdin' out any longer.'

'What happens to the White Sage is none of your business. But what proof do I have? What happened to Rickman and Winthrup?'

'They had a change of plan. Decided to go their own ways.'

Dugmore gave him a suspicious glance. 'I don't know about Winthrup,' he said, 'but Rickman has been with me a long time. Why would he decide to go his own way, as you put it?'

Grote shrugged. 'How should I know? That's their business, not mine.'

'No, your business is killin' people in cold blood,' Dugmore responded with a sudden outburst of annoyance.

Grote shrugged again. 'That's what you ordered, Mr Dugmore.' Something about Grote irritated Dugmore and Grote's next words did little to assuage it.

'I figure on pullin' out myself now the job's done,' he said. 'So if you'll just give me the rest of the money, I'll be on my way.' Although he showed an outward calm, Grote was quite keen to get away from the Sand Ridge area. He knew that three riders were still on his tail. It was unlikely that they would be able to track him as far as the Bar U, but if they did it seemed sensible to be gone and let Dugmore deal with them.

'I'll tell you when you can leave,' Dugmore said, 'and right now isn't the time. I might have more work for you to do.'

'You owe me, Mr Dugmore.'

At his words Johnson stepped forward but Dugmore stopped him with a glance.

'You shall have your money,' he said

to Grote. Getting to his feet, he went though a doorway into a room beyond and returned after a few moments with a wad of cash in his hand.

'Here,' he said, 'take it. I don't go back on my word. But you stay right here till I say you can leave.'

Grote's face was black with suppressed anger, but he was sensible enough to realize there was nothing to be gained by arguing with Dugmore. After all, he didn't need Dugmore's permission to leave. He could ride out any time.

'You'd better be tellin' me the truth about what happened at the White Sage,' Dugmore said. 'My representative will be paying a visit there, and he'll be reporting back.'

He turned away as an indication that the interview was over. When Grote had left he sat for some time thinking about what the gunman had said. It had probably been a mistake hiring him, but there was nothing he could do about that now and there was every likelihood that he might need to call on his services again.

If his latest offer for the White Sage was rejected, it would be an indication that the time had come to take more stringent measures. He didn't really believe Grote's story about Winthrup and Rickman, but it was of little consequence to him what had happened to them. All he was concerned about was getting his new Pony Express enterprise off the ground and acquiring the White Sage. As well as being a desirable property in its own right, it would make the route considerably shorter; in the meantime his riders would just have to go the long way round.

It was late in the afternoon when Caird and his two companions rode into Sand Ridge. They made their way to the livery stables and when they had seen that their horses were catered for, they made their way to the Eastwater Hotel and booked themselves in for a couple of nights. Caird was persuaded that after so many days on the trail, it made sense to take the opportunity to rest up and recuperate. In the evening they made their way to the

Marietta Eating House.

'I reckon I could eat a horse,' Horner said.

Marietta smiled. 'Horse is off the menu today,' she said, 'but if you boys are hungry I could do you a real slap-up grill.'

'Sounds good to me,' Horner replied.

Caird looked up at her. 'Open kind of late?' he queried.

'Not really. The place is quiet at the moment, but there's nothin' else I got to do.'

'Is it always quiet?' Caird replied.

'Not always, but then the marshal keeps a tight lid on things. If there's trouble, it tends to be on the other side of town towards the river landing. I think he likes to keep it that way.'

'That where the rowdy element tends to congregate?' Kitson said.

'Yes. There's a saloon goes by the name of Logan's. If there's any trouble, that's where it's likely to kick off.'

When she had gone Caird turned to the others. 'Once we've finished here,' he said, 'I figure we might pay a little visit to Logan's.'

'If we're gonna learn anythin' about Grote, I guess that's as good a place as any to start,' Horner replied.

When Marietta appeared with the food, they weren't disappointed. To wash down the grill they had a pot of strong black coffee. As they ate, another customer came through the door and took a place at a table opposite. He eyed them surreptitiously and it occurred to Caird that they must look conspicuous. Was there a slight look of apprehension in his glance? If so, what was there about Sand Ridge to cause it? Maybe, after all the hard riding they had done, they looked more like the sort of people he would have expected to find at Logan's rather than the Marietta Eating House.

The man left after a time and shortly after they followed him. They were feeling a lot better for the food and the coffee. There were still people about on the streets but they couldn't help noticing that they tended to give them a wide berth. They came to the plank bridge and walked across it. They could immediately see that the area was run-down and the change in atmosphere was palpable. It was easy to find Logan's. The sound of voices and the tinkling of a piano led them to the batwing doors. A number of horses were tied to the hitch rack outside and Kitson halted and took a few moments to examine their hoofs.

'I figured there was just a chance I might recognize the horse from the hoof prints we followed,' he said.

'Well, do you?'

'Nope. It was just a thought.'

They turned and went through the batwings. One glance was sufficient to tell them what sort of place it was. Although it was comparatively quiet, the air was fetid with sweat and the aroma of soiled sawdust, grime, and stale tobacco. They moved forward through the smoke towards a group of three men in sweat-stained gear. One man's hand was swathed in a dirty bandage. The barman's look was blank.

'Whiskey,' Caird said, putting his foot

on the rail. He glanced in the mirror. It was cracked and caused the reflections to be distorted. However, there was no mistaking the look of hostility on the face of the man with the bandage, and his two companions were equally tough-looking. Caird had a sudden inspiration. They had speculated that maybe Grote had an outlaw roost somewhere. Perhaps they needed to look no further then Logan's Saloon. Certainly, the clientele seemed to match. Caird had the feeling that if the man's hand had not been injured, he might have been more aggressive. How had he come by his injury? His tied-down guns suggested he wasn't a typical range rider. Caird's eyes caught those of Horner in the mirror. They seemed to convey that the oldster was thinking the same. For a moment Caird considered really putting the cat among the pigeons by mentioning Grote's name but almost immediately thought better of it. They had found out enough. Logan's would certainly merit another visit, but for the present there was nothing to be gained by pushing the situation. If Grote was a frequenter of Logan's, there was no point in alerting him to their presence. With the slightest of nods towards the reflected image of the oldster, he threw back the last of his whiskey and turned to go. All the way to the batwings he was conscious that the eyes of the three at the bar were on them. He half expected trouble but there was no further response. The batwings swung behind them as the air outside hit their faces like a cold douche. Kitson bent down to take another look at the horses tethered outside.

'You've already done that,' Horner said.

'Yeah, but then I was lookin' to see if I might recognize Grote's horse. Now I'm takin' a look at the brands.'

After a few moments he straightened up. 'Three of them are carryin' a Bar U brand,' he said. 'I'd call that interestin'.'

'Especially if they belong to the three at the bar,' Caird said. Instead of turning in the direction of town, they walked down to the river landing.

'Are you thinkin' what I'm thinkin'?'

Horner said.

'I reckon so. Logan's is just the sort of place Grote might choose to hang out.'

They relapsed into silence. It was a relief to be out of the saloon and they were enjoying the cool night air as it blew along the river. The sky was filled with stars which were reflected in its dark waters lapping against the pilings. It came almost as a shock when Caird suddenly spoke again.

'We'll keep a watch on Logan's,' he said, 'but I figure it might be worth payin' a visit to the Bar U as well.'

'You know,' Kitson added, 'I was thinkin' the same thing myself.'

$$\star \quad \star \quad \star$$

Following his interview with Grote, which had temporarily irritated him, things had gone well for Dugmore. His two backers, Hobley and Trimble, had finally come up with the money and it was now sitting securely in the bank. In addition, Senator Robertson had virtually guaranteed official backing. As a consequence, he was in a position to finalize the arrangements and set the whole machinery of the Dugmore and Company Overland Mail into operation. A date was set for the first run and advertising for the event was already posted all over town. He intended making a real show of it and the response of the townsfolk had been more than he could have expected. It seemed the old lure of bread and circuses never palled. There was a palpable atmosphere of expectancy around the town.

To top all that, it seemed that things were moving in his direction, too, with regards to the White Sage spread. He had heard from his representative and it seemed Grote had not been lying. The owner of the ranch was absent and he had presented his offer to the foreman who had been left in charge. Obviously, the foreman was in no position to say either yea or nay, but the fact that the owner was not at home was a good sign in itself. From Dugmore's perspective, it meant things were moving along. The man was probably away consulting with his lawyer. It would probably be too much to assume the White Sage would be his before the first Pony Express riders set out. They would have to take the longer route, but it wouldn't take much time till the cut-off became available. If things went really well, he might acquire the White Sage's herd at a knockdown price. The beeves were mostly rounded up and ready to go. It would be particularly piquant if he were to step in at the last moment when the cattle had been trail-herded all the way to market by the White Sage ranch hands. All in all, it was time to celebrate, and with an evil gleam in his eye he awaited the arrival of the young waitress he had falsely summoned to his room. Just then there was a knock on the door.

'Come in!' he shouted, but there was no response. Getting to his feet, he walked across and opened it. Miranda Glover stood outside.

'Ah,' Dugmore said, 'here you are.' His eyes roved over her girlish frame. 'No need to be shy. Why don't you come on in?' She was looking down at her feet and when she glanced up there was a fearful look in her eyes.

'Come in,' Dugmore repeated, and when she still showed hesitancy he took her arm and drew her into the room after him. On an ormolu table a bottle of wine reclined in an ice bucket. 'Why don't you take a seat and make yourself comfortable?' Dugmore said. Turning away, he went over to the table and began to pour the wine when he felt a slight puff of air and, swinging round, saw the door standing ajar. With a curse he put the bottle down and rushed to it, just in time to see the girl as she began to descend the stair.

'Where the hell do you think you're going!' he shouted. The harshness in his voice made her hesitate and in an instant he had covered the ground between them and seized her by the shoulder.

'Oh no,' he hissed, 'you're not going anywhere.'

She opened her mouth to scream but the sound was stifled as he clapped his hand across it. He began to drag her back towards his room. She started to struggle but she was powerless against his brute strength. He forced her into the room and threw her on a settee where she lay sobbing. Her helpless attitude only served to inflame his desire.

'I've had enough of playing games,' he said.

She cowered away as he sat beside her, but he seized her and forced her head backwards till his lips were on hers. He laid one hand on her breast and began to tear at her dress with the other. She was struggling hard now and for a moment he was off balance. She broke free and staggered towards the door, but she didn't get far before he had flung himself upon her. She went down with Dugmore on top of her. Pressing her arms down with a firm grip, he lowered his head, seeking her lips again. He moved one hand and began to reach down, trying to force her legs apart, but suddenly he reeled back. With her arm free she had ripped his cheek with her nails. Instinctively he reached up to feel the wound and she managed to throw him off. In an instant she had regained her feet and was making for the door. He reached out a hand and grabbed her skirt but it ripped and she managed to break free. He struggled to his feet and staggered after her, but his efforts had exhausted him and this time she was too quick. By the time he reached the head of the landing, she had gone.

Breathing heavily, he made his way back to his room and sat down on the settee where he drew out a handkerchief to stem the blood flowing down his face. When he had recovered sufficiently he got back on his feet, made his way to the table and took a long swig of the wine. He needed something stronger. In a cabinet there stood a range of bottles and he poured himself a stiff whiskey. Gradually he regained his composure. Despite this little setback, things had still gone well. His plans were all in order and there was no shortage of other comforts. As for the girl, she wouldn't get away with it. There was no way she could escape him.

Taking her would only be the more sweet for the trouble she had caused him. He would have his revenge. He took another drink and then another and by the time he was part way through the third his thoughts about revenge had coagulated around another issue: the state of affairs with regard to the White Sage. He had given them every chance. If they wouldn't take heed of the latest warning attendant upon Grote's intervention, he would take more stringent measures. Who were these people to stand in his way? A foolish girl and an awkward rancher. No, he had been far too lenient all round. The girl would be his and the White Sage would be his. He would take them both by force. At long last Grote and his fellow gunmen could do something to earn their keep. He should have launched an attack on the White Sage long before this. If the owner did not respond to the latest pressure exerted on his behalf by Grote, he would wait no longer. The White Sage would stand no chance against his array of hired gunslicks. Both the ranch and the girl were already as good as his.

Dugmore wasn't the only one nursing thoughts of revenge. Wheeler, the gunman Buchanan had shot, was not about to forget what had happened to him. He was only waiting for his hand to begin to heal. He had been lucky. The wound wasn't as bad as it might have been because some of the force of the bullet had been deflected by hitting the handle of his own gun.

'How are you gonna find the varmint who did it?' one of his henchmen asked.

Wheeler and his gunslinging companions were passing their time as usual at Logan's.

'That's easy. He said he was makin' for the Saddletree Station. All we got to got to do is take a ride over there.'

His companion scratched his head. 'You know Shefflin?' he asked.

'Sure. Isn't he the old-timer spends most of his time normally hangin' around the bunkhouse?'

'That's the one. Well, he's been seein' people lately wantin' to ride for Dugmore's new Pony Express. Maybe that coyoot was one of 'em.'

Wheeler grinned. 'If that's the case, it's gonna make it all the easier to deal with him.'

'What do you mean?'

'Just what I say. All we got to do is find out which section he's ridin' and we'll be waitin' for him.'

'Mr Dugmore ain't gonna be too pleased if the mail doesn't get through.'

'Maybe not, but he ain't gonna know who was responsible for stoppin' it. Anyway, gettin' shot is just one of the risks those Express riders will be takin'. Not that I intend dealin' with him as simple as that. No, I intend him to suffer for what he done to me.'

His companions could see that Wheeler was beginning to get agitated. 'Take it easy,' one of them said. 'You won't have to wait much longer. From what I hear, Dugmore's just about ready to get that Pony Express shindig up and started. You know that Grote's back?'

'Is that so?'

'Whatever Dugmore asked him to do, seems like he's done it and now everythin' is just about in place.'

Wheeler grinned and turned back to the bartender. 'Set 'em up, Jed. I got a feelin' things are lookin' up.' He glanced down at his bandaged hand and with a slight grimace, flexed the fingers. 'Drink up, boys,' he added.

When Buchanan came down for breakfast on the day he was due to report to Shefflin at the Saddletree Station, he was disappointed not to be served by the young woman the marshal had referred to as Miss Glover. When he had finished, he made his way to the reception desk where the clerk, a pimply youth with a trace of down on his cheeks making pretence to be a beard, lounged with a bored look on his features.

'I was wonderin' if you've seen Miss Glover,' he said.

The youth glanced up at him. 'Miss

Glover don't work here no more,' he said.

Buchanan was surprised at the degree of disappointment he felt. 'Doesn't work here any more,' he repeated. 'Why not? What happened?'

The youth shrugged. 'Seems like she must have been unhappy about somethin'. Or maybe she found somethin' better.'

Buchanan hesitated. Unformed questions gathered in his mind but he couldn't frame them. 'Thanks,' he said, with an attempt at indifference. 'I was just kinda wonderin'.' He made for the door. The sunlight outside and the bustle in the street revived his spirits and by the time he reached the livery stable he was feeling better. After all, this was the day he would receive his final instructions. The time for waiting was over. He would soon be making his first ride for the Pony Express. He was feeling proud.

He mounted his horse and quickly left town. After his encounter with Wheeler, he was a little more careful to avoid straying on to Bar U property, so it was with some surprise that, as he got closer to the Saddletree Station, his keen eyes detected a little cloud of dust out of which three riders presently emerged. They were coming in his direction, but he wasn't about to start running scared. Bringing his horse to a halt, he waited their arrival. As they got closer his keen eyes detected something familiar about one of the riders but it wasn't till they were almost upon him that, with considerable surprise, he finally recognized him as his uncle, the owner of the White Sage.

'Uncle Jess!' he exclaimed. 'What the hell are you doin' here?' Caird looked startled. It was clear he still hadn't recognized his nephew. 'It's me,' Buchanan said. 'Evan, your nephew!'

Suddenly the light dawned in Caird's eyes. 'Evan!' he shouted in return. 'Why, what a turn up for the books!' He turned to his two companions. 'Tarnation, I don't know what's goin' on here, but this is my nephew, Evan Buchanan. The one I told you about.'

In another instant both Caird and

Buchanan had dismounted and were locked in an embrace.

Horner exchanged glances with Kitson. 'At one point he was supposed to be lookin' for the White Sage,' he remarked. 'Looks like the White Sage found him.'

Once Caird and his nephew had recovered from their initial shock, it didn't take long for the explanations.

'I guess it ain't so unusual after all,' Caird commented, when Buchanan had finished his story. 'You takin' on a job with the Pony Express, and us arrivin' in Sand Ridge, I guess it was almost inevitable.'

Horner grinned and spat a globule of phlegm into the dust. 'I guess so,' he remarked aside to Kitson. 'Meetin's like this must be happenin' all the time.'

Caird looked Buchanan up and down closely. 'So you're about to become an Express rider,' he said. 'Well, I don't think it's exactly what your mother had in mind for you, but I suppose it's not everybody could do it. I reckon we should just be thankful that those Paiutes ain't on the warpath for once.'

Buchanan laughed, but quickly became more serious. 'I'm real sorry to hear about what happened back at the White Sage,' he said. 'You say you've tracked the killer right here to Sand Ridge?'

'Not quite all the way, but we've got reason to believe Grote could be around some place.'

'We came across some real mean *hombres* at a place in town called Logan's,' Kitson said. 'They looked like the kind of no-good coyotes someone like Grote might hang about with.'

Buchanan thought for a moment. 'That's funny,' he said. 'I paid a visit to the same place and saw the gunnie I shot in the hand. You say you're checkin' out the Bar U. It's somethin' of a coincidence if he's ridin' for the outfit.'

'What's even more significant is that there seems to be a tie-in between the Bar U and the Overland Mail Company.'

'You mean Dugmore?'

'Exactly. I don't suppose you've come across him?'

'Only the name,' Buchanan said.

Kitson gave the youngster a shrewd glance. 'I don't know,' he said, 'but it looks to me like you might have got yourself into somethin' takin' on this job.'

Buchanan nodded. 'Maybe so, but that reminds me; I need to get goin'. I've got an appointment at the Saddletree Station. How about we meet up later? There are a whole lot of things we got to catch up on.'

'Sure,' Caird said. 'There's a nice eating place in town called Marietta's; or there's the hotel.'

Buchanan looked from one to the other of them. 'Marietta's is fine,' he said. 'At least, to start with.'

'What do you mean by that?' Caird asked.

'Well, didn't Kitson just say Logan's was the sort of place you might run into Grote?'

'You've got a point,' Caird said.

'It could be a real interestin' evening,' Horner commented.

Buchanan walked across to his horse and swung into the saddle. 'OK,' he said,

'I'll see you boys later.'

'Less of the 'boys',' Caird said, and then added, 'at the Marietta Eating House.'

Buchanan rode way. As he went, he turned over in his mind what his uncle had told him. Was there a connection between Dugmore and Grote? There was no denying that Wheeler and his fellow gunnies were associated with Dugmore, but that could be explained away. After all, a man couldn't always be held to account for the behaviour of his employees. But if Grote was indeed one of them, it begged the question what Dugmore's motives would be in having him ride as far as the White Sage. Was Dugmore ultimately responsible for what had happened there?

He was still thinking over these matters when the station came into view. He rode into the yard and dismounted. There was only one other horse at the hitch-rail, a handsome palomino. He had been expecting other Express riders to congregate there. In a few moments the figure of Shefflin appeared on the veranda.

'Am I the only one?' Buchanan asked.

'Yup. There's a reason for that.'

'What would that be?'

'If you care to step inside you'll find out.'

Buchanan gave the oldster a puzzled glance before stepping up on the veranda. Shefflin turned and preceded him into the building. Peering beyond him, Buchanan could see a portly figure sitting at the table. Once they were inside Shefflin turned back to him.

'Buchanan,' he said, 'meet Mr Dugmore.'

Buchanan was taken aback but tried not to show his surprise. Instead, bearing in mind the recent conversation with his uncle, he concentrated on observing his new employer. He was a burly man who wore a black frock-coat and a patterned waistcoat. His otherwise sparse hair was oddly long at the back. He got to his feet as Shefflin stepped aside.

'Mr Buchanan, isn't it?' he said. 'I'm pleased to make your acquaintance.' He held out his hand and Buchanan advanced to take it.

'Mr Shefflin has told me something about you. It seems he was impressed with your riding.'

Buchanan wasn't sure how to respond. 'You've got some mighty fine horses,' he replied, somewhat lamely.

'We have indeed,' Dugmore said, 'and a whole lot of other things too. Fine horses, fine men, good equipment. Do you know what it takes to run just one station? Apart from the cost of actually building it?'

Again, Buchanan wasn't sure what to answer so didn't say anything and let Dugmore run on.

'A station keeper, a stock tender; sometimes more. Two to five horses at each station. Food, housekeeping, even medicine. It all has to be freighted across rough terrain. Yes sir, it's a big operation.'

'I'm mighty proud to be picked as one of the riders,' Buchanan said.

'Well, I'm real pleased to hear you say that, because do you know what I consider the most valuable asset for one of my employees?' Buchanan's mind was blank. 'Loyalty,' Dugmore concluded. 'Loyalty to the brand.' He turned to Shefflin. 'Ain't that so?' he said.

'Sure is,' Shefflin replied.

'Mr Shefflin knows. That's why he's been with me for so long. He knows the value of loyalty. And loyalty means, in this case, that the mail gets through no matter what. Do you understand me? First the mail, and then everythin' else a long way behind. You got him to sign the Declaration, Shefflin?'

'Sure thing,' Shefflin replied.

'Read that through and take it to heart,' Dugmore said. 'Always remember: the mail comes first, your horse second, and the rider last.'

'I understand, Mr Dugmore,' Buchanan said. 'Believe me, you can count on me.'

Dugmore waited for a moment, looking hard at Buchanan, before settling back in his chair. 'Well,' he said, 'I won't keep you in suspense any longer. The inaugural ride of the Dugmore and Company Overland

Mail is set for three days' time, and the first rider to carry the mail will be you.'

Buchanan's earlier suspicions about Dugmore were temporarily forgotten as he felt a surge of pride and excitement course through his veins. 'Thanks, Mr Dugmore,' he said. 'Be sure, I won't let you down.'

In response Dugmore got to his feet and proffered his hand once more to Buchanan. He turned to his assistant. 'I need to go now. Mr Shefflin will fill you in on all the details. Just be sure you're prepared and ready to ride.'

'Thanks again,' Buchanan mumbled.

With a final nod, Dugmore made his way outside, mounted the palomino, and rode away. Shefflin and Buchanan watched him from the door frame.

'Well, son,' Shefflin said, 'looks like you made an impression.'

Buchanan had a feeling that he owed his favourable treatment at least in part to the oldster. 'Thanks for puttin' in a word for me,' he said.

'Don't thank me,' Shefflin replied. 'You

got a hard ride in front of you and by the time this is all over, you might be thinkin' differently.'

'What do you mean, by the time it's all over?'

'Just an expression,' Shefflin said. 'After all, nothin' in this world lasts.' He paused for a moment, as if remembering something, before continuing, 'By the way, I had somebody in here askin' questions about you.'

'Yeah?' Buchanan queried. 'Who was it?'

'Someone it would have been best not to antagonize, someone carryin' a damaged hand.'

'That varmint who set on me the first time I was out here?'

'Yes, Wheeler. Don't worry, I didn't give anything away, but he knows enough. And if he didn't know beforehand, he only has to turn up in town the day after tomorrow to see who's deliverin' the mail.'

'Thanks for lettin' me know.'

'Whatever the situation between you and Wheeler, I don't want to know. It ain't none of my business. But I never took to Wheeler, or any of his cronies for that matter. And he ain't the sort to forget a grudge.' There was a pause before Shefflin continued, 'Let's go outside and take another look at those horses. Then I can explain anythin' else you need to know.'

Buchanan grinned. 'I reckon I already know what horse to choose, if I get a choice, that is.'

'You get a choice,' Shefflin replied. Together, they made their way to the corral.

Caird and his companions did not spend too long reconnoitring the Bar U after running into Buchanan. One thing they did was to check the brands on the few cattle that they ran across. In each case the Bar U brand appeared to be genuine and there were no others.

'Whatever this Dugmore *hombre* might be about, rustlin' don't seem to be part of it,' Horner commented.

'Not on the basis of what we've seen

of these critters,' Caird agreed, 'but they can only be a fraction of what Dugmore must be runnin'.'

Kitson glanced all about him. 'No sign of any welcomin' committee for us,' he said. 'Maybe your nephew was just unlucky.'

'Maybe,' Horner remarked.

'I reckon we should head back to town,' Caird said. 'So far we haven't got any evidence that Grote is in the area, much less that he's ridin' for Dugmore. If Grote is around, I figure we'll be more likely to hear of him at Logan's.'

'I agree,' Horner said. 'Who knows? We might even be lucky enough to catch him there this time.'

Caird was thoughtful. 'Maybe I owe it to his mother to keep Evan away from the place,' he mused.

'There's no point in thinkin' that way. Besides, he suggested goin' there himself. There's no way you could keep him away if he once decided to go.'

After a moment Caird nodded. 'I guess you're right.'

'Of course I'm right. But I figure he can look after himself.'

'Look at it his way,' Kitson said. 'If trouble develops, whether it's at Logan's or anywhere else, it's better if he's got us right alongside him.'

Kitson's argument seemed to clinch the matter. Satisfied that there was nothing else to be gained by remaining in the vicinity of the Bar U, they turned and set their course for Sand Ridge to await Buchanan's return.

5

Sand Ridge was the sort of place where trouble could quickly brew and just as quickly spread. Marshal Bedford had his own methods for keeping a lid on things. That was why he chose not to do very much about cleaning up the seedier part of town towards the river. That was where trouble, if it came, was likely to occur, and he could isolate it there. Logan's saloon was at the centre of it, and he kept a close eye on its clientele. But the marshal didn't just devote all his time and attention to knowing what was going on in and around town. He also liked to keep a finger on the pulse of what was happening in the surrounding district, and in particular the Bar U. He was no fool. He was fully aware that Dugmore was not the honest upright citizen he made himself out to be. So long as he did nothing overtly unlawful, he was prepared to turn a blind eye to Dugmore's various business activities, but he was aware that Dugmore employed some very dubious characters, which suggested that some of his schemes were, at the very least, somewhat shady. He had his sources of information to keep him abreast of developments at the Bar U, so it was with interest that he stood outside his office and observed one of his informants, a Bar U ranch hand by name of Worley, come riding down the main street. He drew his horse to a halt and lowered himself from the saddle.

'Howdy, Marshal,' he said.

Bedford sensed that Worley's business was with him, so he quickly led the way inside.

'You look like you could do with a drink,' he said.

As Worley took a seat, he produced a bottle and a couple of glasses and poured them both whiskey.

'How are things at the Bar U?' the marshal asked, when they had taken a swig.

'That's what I've come to see you

about,' Worley replied.

'Go ahead.'

'Well, I don't know exactly what's goin' on, but there's a whole lot of activity at the Bar U right now. From what I can discover, a bunch of Dugmore's men are gettin' ready for somethin'.'

'Any idea what it's about?'

'No, but from what I can gather they're preparin' for a long ride.'

'You're sure it isn't somethin' to do with the openin' of the Pony Express service?'

'I guess it could be, but I don't think so. There's somethin' else afoot. And most of the ones gettin' involved are those hard-cases Dugmore has taken on recently.'

The marshal took another drink. 'That's real interestin',' he said. 'I don't suppose you have any idea where they might be headed?'

'Nope.'

'Just so long as they ain't thinkin' of hittin' town,' the marshal said. 'That's the main thing that concerns me. I wonder what Dugmore could be up to? He's got plenty on his hands already.'

'I don't know,' Worley said. 'I just figured you'd be interested. I thought you ought to know.'

'You were right,' the marshal said. 'Thanks for comin' in to tell me.'

'I'd better get goin',' Worley said, laying down his glass and getting to his feet. The marshal escorted him to the door.

'If you see or hear anythin' else, I'd sure appreciate if you let me know,' he said.

He didn't wait around while Worley swung into leather and rode off again. He had something to think about. Was there any significance in what Worley had told him? If so, what did it portend? Maybe nothing so far as the township of Sand Ridge was directly concerned, but it was worth further investigation. In the meantime, he had another little job to do. Three strangers had hit town and registered at the Eastwater Hotel. They were not youngsters with a potential to cause trouble, but it was his custom to introduce himself to any newcomers just to let them know he was around.

Wheeler was not in a good mood when he returned in the evening to the Bar U bunkhouse. Although he tried to make himself scarce, there were times when he couldn't avoid having to do some jobs around the place. In view of the fact that his hand was still not entirely recovered, he had been assigned some light duties around the stables. The day was hot and so was his temper. Before he had even completed his tasks, he strode out of the stable and stormed into the bunkhouse and flung himself down on his mattress. For a while he lay staring at the ceiling. His anger was unfocused but soon it began to gather round the thought of Buchanan and the little matter of revenge. He was still thinking about it when the door was flung open and one of his drinking companions from Logan's appeared. He looked at Wheeler as if surprised to see him.

'What are you starin' at?' Wheeler snapped.

'I didn't expect to find you here. I

figured you'd be with Grote and his gang.'

It was Wheeler's turn to look surprised.

'You know they're getting' ready to ride? On Dugmore's orders?'

'Is that right? How many of 'em?'

'More than a dozen. I figure it's got somethin' to do with that White Sage spread Dugmore's been after. Grote's not long been back from the same place. The way I see it, Dugmore's finally about to make his move.'

Wheeler made an effort to sit up. 'Whatever it's about, it doesn't interest me. I never took to Grote anyway. He thinks he's a big noise, but that's all it is: noise. I'm just as pleased to see the back of him.'

His companion grunted. He took a close look at Wheeler and then continued, 'I've got some other news. Guess who's gonna be the first rider for Dugmore's Pony Express?' Wheeler looked blank. 'None other than your friend Buchanan.' The mention of Buchanan's name brought Wheeler to his senses.

'Buchanan?' he said. 'You're sure about that?'

'It's the word around the Bar U.'

In contrast with his previous stupor, Wheeler's brain was suddenly surprisingly active. 'When's it happenin'?' he asked.

'Hell, don't you know? Dugmore has been spreadin' the word and the town's gettin' ready for a regular carnival. It's set for the day after tomorrow.'

Wheeler's brow was creased in thought. He had already forgotten about Grote and his posse.

'What's the name of the first station out from here?' he asked.

'I think the nearest home station is Indian Flat.'

'That must be seventy miles away or more. Ain't there somethin' nearer?'

'There must be at least a couple of relay stations between Sand Ridge and Indian Flat. I guess the nearest one would be Dead Tree Creek.'

Wheeler seemed to weigh up the man's words. After a few moments the frown written across his features was replaced by a broad grin. 'How do you and Quint fancy takin' a little ride?' he asked. The man looked puzzled. 'Let me spell it out,' Wheeler said. 'Buchanan has to stop at Dead Tree Creek to change horses. Well, there'll be a little reception committee waitin' there to greet him: me, you and Quint.'

The man's face didn't register any response.

'You haven't forgotten what Buchanan did to me?' Wheeler rasped. He held up his hand. A light of understanding began to dawn in the man's eyes.

'Yeah, I think I see what you mean,' he said. He thought for a moment. 'But won't there be someone there already?'

'Yeah. There'll be a station keeper, maybe even a stock tender as his assistant. But it's a dangerous job. Those Paiutes just ain't to be trusted.'

'Dugmore ain't gonna like it.'

'The hell with Dugmore. What do we care about the mail? Anyway, there are plenty of other riders. It won't amount to more than a glitch to him.'

'I wasn't just thinkin' about the mail.'

'You're worryin' about those station

hands? Like I say, it's a risky business. If it ain't Paiutes on the warpath, it's horse rustlers or outlaws.' He suddenly smirked. 'Hell, if that's all that's botherin' you, we can bushwhack Buchanan before he even reaches the place.'

The man's expression was still doubtful but he looked up to Wheeler and Buchanan had insulted them all. Suddenly he grinned. 'I'll let Quint know.'

'I'll tell Quint. Just make sure you keep your mouth shut. Nobody else needs to know. This is our affair.'

The man sat on his bunk and Wheeler walked to the door and went outside. He was feeling a whole lot better now than he had when he first entered the bunkhouse. Things had turned out well. He had been weighing up how to deal with Buchanan without arriving at any definite decision, but now things seemed to be working in his favour. He had come up with a plan, a good plan. It only remained to work out a few details; like making sure they left in plenty of time to reach the Dead

Tree Creek relay station well ahead of Buchanan and were ready and waiting for him there.

Evening had fallen on Sand Ridge and in the bar of the Eastwater Hotel, Caird and his companions were awaiting the arrival of Buchanan.

'I still don't know what his ma would make of it all,' Caird said, addressing them, 'but I got to admit that I, for one, am proud of the boy.'

'You got good reason,' Horner said.

'I propose a toast,' Caird said. 'To my nephew Buchanan and the Pony Express.'

'Shouldn't we wait till he arrives?'

Caird glanced out of the window. 'Could be any time,' he said. 'I got a good view of Marietta's from here. I'll see him when he appears.'

'That reminds me,' Horner said. 'I'm gettin' kinda hungry.'

They downed their glasses and Caird was about to refill them when he became aware of a slight stir in the atmosphere. He looked up to see that a man had entered and was approaching their table. On his chest he wore a shining tin star.

'Howdy, Marshal,' he said.

'Howdy,' the marshal replied. 'Mind if I join you?' Without waiting for a reply, he took a spare seat from an adjoining table and sat down beside them.

'Care for a drink?' Horner asked.

'Not for me.' There was a slight pause before the marshal went on. 'I don't intend takin' up much of your time. You'll understand that when a group of folks arrive in town like yourselves, I like to know their business.'

'That's easy,' Caird replied. 'In fact, we were plannin' on payin' you a visit. Maybe you can help us. We're looking for a man called Grote. Maybe you've heard of him. He's an outlaw and a known gunslinger.'

If the name registered with Bedford, he wasn't showing it. 'This is a quiet town,' he said. 'I'd like to keep it that way.'

'Maybe you'd better tell him what Grote did,' Horner suggested.

The marshal looked across at him. 'That sounds like a good idea,' he said.

Trying to keep the story as brief as possible, Caird outlined what had happened at the White Sage and subsequently. When he had finished the marshal looked at him searchingly.

'So you got no good reason to suppose that this *hombre* Grote is actually here in Sand Ridge?'

'No. We trailed him most of the way. It seemed a fair deduction.'

Bedford looked Caird in the eye. 'You say you're the owner of the White Sage?'

'That's right.'

'Then you must be the uncle of a young feller called Buchanan.' The marshal had thrown in the name in order to observe what effect it might have and he wasn't disappointed. The startled look on the faces of Caird and his companions was enough to assure him that their story was true.

'You've met my nephew?' Caird finally managed to say.

'Yup. He had a spot of trouble with some hardcases, but from what I can gather he handled it OK.'

Caird glanced at Horner and Kitson. It was his turn to throw in a name. 'Those hardcases seemed to be workin' for an outfit called the Bar U. Apparently it's run by a man named Dugmore. Maybe you could tell us a little bit more about him.'

The marshal grinned. 'That's easy enough. I expect you've made the connection with the Dugmore and Company Overland Express. I hope your nephew knows who's on his side and who isn't.'

'The town seems to be gettin' excited,' Kitson remarked. 'The inaugural ride is tomorrow and Buchanan is doin' it.'

It seemed to Kitson that the marshal was about to respond but he was suddenly silent.

Caird observed him closely. 'Somethin' wrong?' he enquired.

Bedford was thinking hard. He seemed to have been struck by a new idea. He looked from Caird to his companions. 'You've got your suspicions about Dugmore. So have I. You tell me that someone is applying a lot of pressure for you to sell up. Well, it's probably occurred to you already, but it would certainly be to Dugmore's benefit to have control of the White Sage. Apart from anythin' else, it could be right in the way of his preferred Pony Express route.'

Caird nodded. 'Dugmore certainly seems to employ some dubious characters,' he said. 'It wouldn't be beyond the bounds of possibility that Grote is one of them.'

The marshal gave him a hard look. 'Things are startin' to fit,' he said. 'Listen. I just got word earlier that Dugmore is linin' up a bunch of his hardcases ready for a ride. I was wonderin' where they might be headed. It just occurs to me that they might be headin' for the White Sage.'

It was Caird's turn to think hard. 'It would figure,' he said. 'When are they leavin'?'

'I don't have that information, but my guess is that it would be tomorrow right about the time your nephew takes off with the mail.'

'Then we got to do somethin' about

stallin' 'em,' Caird said. 'Can we count on your assistance?'

'My responsibility is to the town,' Bedford replied. 'If anythin' is goin' on involvin' you and Dugmore, it ain't none of my business.'

'If we're right about all this,' Horner interposed, 'then it becomes your business. If Dugmore gets away with employin' gunslingers and murderers to carry out his business, the town won't be safe. The only way to make sure Dugmore doesn't become an even bigger threat than he is now is to deal with him before things get out of hand.'

'You know,' Bedford said, 'I think you're right. So far I've kept this town a place for decent folk to live by playin' it softly. It's worked, so far, but I reckon that approach ain't goin' to answer much longer. The place needs cleanin' out.'

There was a pause and Caird took the opportunity to glance again out of the window. Coming down the street he saw Buchanan making his way to the Marietta Eating House.

'There's my nephew now,' he said. 'We arranged to meet him at Marietta's.'

'Listen,' the marshal said. 'I got business to attend to. Why don't you come down to my office early tomorrow mornin'? I mean around sunup. We can decide then what we do about Dugmore.'

'Sounds good to me,' Caird said. They all rose from the table together and made their way outside.

'See you in the mornin',' Bedford said.

'Sure thing,' Caird replied. The marshal walked away and Caird watched him for a moment before turning to the others.

'Evan's gone into Marietta's,' he said. 'We'd better get across there and join him, but don't say anythin' about our conversation with the marshal. He's got the ride tomorrow and it wouldn't do any good to burden him with it. Whatever happens with the Bar U, we can deal with it.'

'That sounds sensible,' Kitson said. 'Leastways, as sensible as any of the rest of it.'

Horner took a glance in the direction of the eating house. 'I don't know about you boys,' he said, 'but I'm gettin' mighty hungry.'

They crossed to the restaurant. Buchanan had not long taken his seat as they came through the door.

'I got somethin' to tell you,' he said, as they joined him at the table.

'Let's order first,' Caird said.

'Good thinkin',' Horner added.

They looked around for Marietta. Just at that moment the door to the kitchen opened and instead of Mariettta another young woman appeared. She halted by the counter and Caird was preparing to speak for them if she should come over when his attention was drawn to his nephew. His mouth had fallen open and there was a startled expression on his blanched face.

'Do you know the young lady?' Caird asked.

Buchanan nodded. 'She used to work at the hotel,' he said.

Caird observed him closely and

recognized the signs. *Aha*, he thought, *the young whippersnapper certainly hasn't been wasting his time*. Further speculation was halted when Marietta appeared and they both approached the table.

'Hello, boys,' Marietta said. 'It's nice to see you all.'

'It's quiet again,' Caird replied.

'Then it's a good time for me to introduce my new waitress, Miss Miranda Glover. She only just started this very evening. You're almost her first customers.'

Caird glanced at the girl. Her eyes were resting on Buchanan. He seemed to have recovered some of his aplomb as he remarked, 'I think Miss Glover and I have met before. At the Eastwater Hotel.'

'That wouldn't be surprising. Miranda worked there till recently but now she is with me.'

The young woman summoned up a faint smile. 'I think I will like it here much better,' she said. 'The Eastwater vacancy was only temporary.'

'I'm just showing Miranda the ropes,' Marietta said. She turned again to her protégée. 'Can I leave you to take these gentlemen's orders?' she asked.

'Yes,' Miranda answered.

While she was taking their orders, Buchanan watched her surreptitiously. He sensed rather than felt that she was doing the same with him. He wondered what the story was behind her leaving the Eastwater Hotel to work at Marietta's. He had a feeling that there was more to the older woman's solicitation for her new waitress than met the eye. He couldn't be certain, but there seemed to be a slight discolouration to the girl's left cheek. It was hard to put a finger on what was bothering him, but this time he didn't mean to waste the opportunity the situation had presented of getting better acquainted with her at last. He glanced at his three, to him, ageing companions. There wasn't much he could do while they were around, but he would find the occasion to talk to her. He felt more confident since his promotion to being a star rider with the Pony Express and he wasn't looking to be leaving it in a hurry. No, he would be around. Time was on his side. He took another look at his uncle. There seemed to be a slight smile hovering about his features and there was a quizzical look in his eye. Then, suddenly, he felt an odd lowering of the emotional temperature. The Pony Express was owned by Dugmore. Didn't he also own the Eastwater Hotel? Again, there was nothing definite he could have put a finger on, but he sensed a vague and strange intimation of menace. He was so rapt in the troubling sensation that he failed to register his uncle's voice remarking *Didn't you say you had something to tell us?* until he had repeated it twice.

The inauguration day for the Dugmore and Company Overland Mail Express had finally arrived and Dugmore had made sure the town of Sand Ridge was in a mood to celebrate. The Eastwater Hotel was thronged with guests. Flags were fluttering in the breeze and bunting draped the wooden canopies of the stores along Main Street and the river landing.

The steamboat that had brought the mail up the river was tied up there while its crew and passengers enjoyed the proceedings. When Buchanan appeared leading a bay mustang, the crowd erupted into a frenzy of clapping and cheering. Some of them surged forward and, pressing round the somewhat bemused young man, attempted to pluck hairs from the horse's mane to weave into rings and watch chains as souvenirs. Overhead, Dugmore watched the proceedings from a room behind the balcony of the hotel, accompanied by his two backers, Hobley and Trimble. Senator Robertson himself had made the journey to Sand Ridge on the steamer and all four of them were looking very pleased with themselves.

'Well, Dugmore,' the senator said, 'it sure looks like your Pony Express venture has caught the public imagination.'

'I told you, boys; it's a sure-fire scheme. Sand Ridge is gonna be right up there with St Joseph or even Chicago. You just wait and see.'

'Steady!' the senator replied. 'It's all

looking very good, but let's not get ahead of ourselves.'

A brass band began to play martial music and they stopped to listen. Buchanan had brought the mustang round to the front of the hotel and, despite all the claims to his attention, he couldn't help looking out for the trim figure of Miranda Glover. He wanted her to see him in his uniform of blue shirt and pants, fringed buckskin jacket and high boots. He looked in the direction of the Marietta Eating House. At first he was disappointed, but when he looked again the door opened and Miranda emerged. His heart seemed to skip a beat. She stood for a moment and then she gave a discreet wave. It took him a moment to realize it was aimed at him before he waved back. She waited a little while longer and then turned and went back inside. Gathering himself together, he glanced at the face of his silver-cased watch; only a quarter of an hour to go. Not for the first time he checked the horse over. The *mochila* lay across the saddle, its cantinas carrying the precious letters as well as copies of the *Sand Ridge Courier*.

The brass-band music came to a halt and Dugmore appeared on the balcony. He raised an arm as though in salute; the gathered crowd looked up and the general hubbub gradually ceased.

'Ladies and gentlemen, today we are all privileged to be present at an historic moment in the history of these United States. Today our town of Sand Ridge is at the focus of the onward march of civilization and progress.'

In the room behind him, the senator glanced at his two companions. 'Layin' it on a bit thick, ain't he?' he muttered.

'It don't hurt to get folks fired up,' Hobley replied.

Dugmore's words continued to ring out and when he finally reached the end of his speech, it was greeted by a roar from the crowd. From the direction of the river a cannon boomed; the stern-wheeler moored at the dock sounded its siren and gunshots cracked and sang as a few excited citizens fired their guns into the air.

At the signal Buchanan swung into the saddle. Feeling more than a little self-conscious, he raised his Stetson to the crowd and began to edge his mount down the dusty street. He looked around, searching for his uncle and his companions without success. He felt a slight twinge of disappointment but consoled himself with the reflection that they were probably watching the proceedings even though he couldn't see them. Again, a little shame-facedly, he waved his Stetson. His horse shied but he quickly had it back under control. He could sense that it was bursting to be set free. The roar of the spectators rang in his ears but gradually began to fade as he reached the end of the main strip. With a last glance back, he applied his spurs to the mustang's flanks and it broke forwards, rapidly moving into a gallop. He felt the strength in its muscles and chest as it ran freely, released from restraint at last. Its hoofs beat out a steady rhythm as the wind blew in his face. He felt a surge of youth and vigour and couldn't resist letting out a whoop of sheer exultation, altogether forgetful of Dugmore and his ambiguous feelings towards him. He was the first rider for the Pony Express and he was right on time.

The early morning sun was just gaining strength as four riders approached the boundary line of the Bar U. They were Marshal Bedford, Caird, Horner and Kitson. They had met up earlier as arranged, but hadn't been able to come up with any positive plans. Their instincts told them that Dugmore was brewing up trouble, but they had nothing definite to go on. A lot of their suspicions were conjecture. They needed something more substantial. If they were to find Grote among the gang of gunslicks reputed to be about to set off on some mission, it would go a long way towards providing the proof they needed that there was indeed a link between Dugmore and recent events at the White Sage. They realized that Dugmore himself would probably be in town, which made it seem perhaps a good time to pay a visit on the Bar U. Caird was turning it all over in his mind when Horner rode up close.

'Pity you'll miss things back in town,' he said. Engrossed in his thoughts, Caird did not realize at first what Horner was talking about.

'I mean your nephew bein' picked to be the first ride for the Pony Express,' Horner said.

'Yeah. I guess he'll be lookin' out for us too. But it's better he isn't distracted by anythin' we might be doin'.'

'I'm not too sure just what that is, but I take your point.'

As they continued riding, they observed cattle standing singly or in small groups, but didn't take any time to check their brands.

'Dugmore seems to be a bit behindhand with the roundup,' Horner remarked.

'I guess he's got other things to think about,' Caird replied.

'We'd better be gettin' back to the White Sage pretty soon ourselves,' the oldster remarked. 'I know Drysdale is holdin' the fort back there, but it's about time our beeves were on the hoof.'

'Seems funny there aren't a few more people around,' Kitson commented. 'For once, they don't seem to be livin' up to their name.'

'How do you mean?' Horner asked.

'The Bar U. There ain't nobody tried to bar us so far.'

They carried on riding, still without meeting anyone, till the Bar U ranch house hove into few.

'Nice place,' Horner remarked.

'Yeah, but there's somethin' about it don't ring true. Looks more like some kinda mansion than a regular ranch.'

They sat their horses, observing the place for a while. Presently someone emerged from the bunkhouse and went into a barn, but apart from that there was no activity.

'Maybe they've all taken the day off to go into town.'

'There's only one way to find out,' Caird said.

Spurring their horses, they rode into the yard. As they dismounted the man they had previously seen appeared round the corner of the building. His keen eyes alighted on the marshal's badge.

'Howdy,' he said. 'Anythin' I can do for you folks?'

Caird glanced at Bedford, who spoke for them all.

'We'd like a word with Dugmore,' he said.

The man's response was to break into a laugh. 'Man, you've sure chosen the wrong day,' he said. 'Don't you know today's the day for the first mail run? You know, the Pony Express? Mr Dugmore's in town and so are a lot of the rest of the boys.'

'Are you the only one left?'

'Just about. Another group rode off earlier. I don't know where they were goin'.'

Caird and the marshal exchanged glances. 'It's not mid-mornin' yet. They left kinda early, didn't they?' Bedford said.

'That's what I thought. I'd probably have missed them except I don't keep so well.'

'How many of 'em?'

'I'd say about a dozen. To be honest, I was glad to see the back of 'em. Mr Dugmore has taken on some mighty ornery folk lately. I don't know why. They don't seem to do anythin' much round here.'

'Does the name Grote mean anythin' to you?' Caird asked.

The man stroked his chin. 'Yeah,' he said. 'As a matter of fact, one of the ranch hands mentioned the name. He even pointed him out to me. He was one of those rode out this mornin'. Like I say, I was glad to see the back of him.'

'Do you know where they were goin?' Bedford asked.

'Nope. I figured it must be somethin' to do with the Pony Express. Maybe they were gonna be involved in the celebrations.'

The marshal looked at Caird; Caird's face was grim. 'I think we know where they're headed,' he muttered.

Bedford turned to the man. 'Thanks,' he said.

The man shrugged. 'Glad to have been of help. Is there anythin' else you boys would like to know?'

'I think we know enough,' Bedford replied.

'Then you'll excuse me,' the man said. 'I don't know what else is goin' on round here, but I got things to do.' As he turned and walked away, Horner turned to Caird.

'What do we do now?' he said.

'I think that's pretty obvious,' Caird replied. 'Those gunslicks have got to be headin' for the White Sage, but they can't be too far ahead of us. If we get on their trail and ride hard, we should catch up with them somewhere along the line.' He faced the marshal. 'What about you?' he said. 'Are you comin' with us?'

The marshal thought for a moment before shaking his head. 'My duty lies here,' he said. 'I figure I need to get back into town and keep an eye on things there. But

I wish you boys well. You realize the three of you will be outnumbered somethin' like four to one even if you succeed in catching up with those *hombres*?'

'We'll have the element of surprise,' Caird replied.

The marshal smiled grimly. 'It doesn't amount to very much to my way of thinkin',' he said, 'but you got your own reasons.'

'We sure have,' Horner responded. 'Come on, we're wastin' time. Let's get after the varmints.'

Without further ado, they turned their horses and took their leave of the Bar U.

6

After the first flush of hard riding, Buchanan slowed his mustang down and carried on riding at an easier pace. He was still conscious of the requirement for speed, but he knew there was no point in letting the horse get blown. The trail stretched a long way ahead, fringed just here by mesquite and greasewood. He reflected that it would have been an advantage if he had ridden the trail before, but there had been no time to do so even if he had known which stretch was to be his. Turning his gaze from the trail ahead, he glanced down at the *mochila* on which he was sitting. It was a clever design; a square leather sheet which was thrown over the saddle, covering it completely. The saddle horn and cantle protruded through slits and a leather *cantina* was sewn into each corner. The four *cantinas* contained the mail and were locked. With no straps to unbuckle, the *mochila* could be transferred from horse to horse in no time at all. He fell to wondering who would be waiting at the relay station to take the mail on to the next change over. Shefflin had mentioned a name but he was damned if he could remember. It made no difference; the mechanics of how the runs were organized was none of his business. To save weight, he carried no rifle, but two Colt revolving pistols were stuck under his belt.

His run was roughly eighty miles to the home station at Indian Flat, but he would be changing horses three times in between. He had a feeling that Dugmore was pushing things. He was expecting a lot of his horses and riders, maybe too much, but Buchanan was determined not to let anyone down. Looking ahead of him once more, he urged the mustang into a gallop. The beast responded to his touch and they tore along, making good ground. Buchanan's only concern was that the horse might run into a hole and fall, but while it was daylight he did not worry unduly. He was riding due west of Sand Ridge and was confident of being able to find his way, but just in case he needed it, he carried a compass in a pocket of his jacket along with the pocket Bible he had been given by Shefflin. That oldster had given him directions to Dead Tree Creek and, as he rode, he looked out for any of the landmarks Shefflin had told him to watch out for. The mustang was eating up the ground but showing no sign of tiredness; when he tried slowing it down again, it showed its irritation by tugging at the bit.

The country was growing rougher and vegetation was sparse, so when he saw the gaunt, twisted shape of a dead tree outlined against the sky like a gallows, he knew he must be getting close to the first relay station. Of the creek there was not a sign, just a dry dusty depression which could once have been a streambed. Straining his eyes for a sight of a building, he soon detected what he was looking for. It didn't amount to much, being nothing more than a crude hut with a thatched roof sodded with earth from which sprang a rank growth of weeds and grass. Adjoining it was a rough stable. He was expected and someone should be on hand, but he couldn't see any signs of activity. He was surprised that the stock-tender wasn't standing by with his change of horse. His remount should be there, ready rigged, in the yard, waiting for the *mochila* to be slung across its saddle.

He looked closely at the cabin. The afternoon was drawing down and it was dark inside. It looked unwelcoming. He slowed down and then brought the mustang to a stop. As he did so there was a flash from inside the cabin followed by the crash of a rifle. Another shot rang out from the direction of the stable, rapidly followed by another one from the cabin. A bullet ricocheted from the pommel of his saddle and as the mustang reared, he felt another cut through the space his body had occupied a moment earlier. He partly jumped and partly fell from the saddle as the mustang bolted. Bullets were ripping the air as he rolled into the brush and flattened himself against the ground. Drawing one of his .44s, he slammed a couple of shots into the wall of the cabin. In reply, flame stabbed from the cabin windows. Raising himself slightly and taking more deliberate aim, he sighted on the flashes and squeezed the trigger. There was an answering scream, ringing out even above the cacophony of gunfire. He waited a moment to see what the effect might be. For a few seconds the barrage from the cabin ceased, but then it resumed as a shot rang out and a bullet whined past not far over his head. On his belly, he crawled further to his right, hoping that the movement would be unobserved. Shots were coming from the direction of the stable and he tried to work out how many of the gunmen he was up against; his best estimate was not more than a couple in either building. From his new position, he opened fire again till his gun was empty.

There was a lull in the exchange; lying on his back, he reloaded as quickly as he could. As he did so, he considered whether he should try making a break. It would be extreme risky, but if there was a chance he could reach the runaway mustang, it could be a risk worth taking. He took a deep breath and started to rise when there was another burst of gunfire and he sank back again. His movement had brought him closer to the side of the stable. After a moment's thought he decided to try and get behind the buildings. If he succeeded in doing so, he might be out of sight. He looked up at the sky. Dusk was descending. It might serve to provide some cover. He crawled forward a little further and then, bracing himself, leaped to his feet and, doubled over, began to sprint. His move was met by a rattle of gunfire and bullets ripped up the ground in front of him. He veered and swerved, running as hard as he could, till he reached a point parallel to the side of the building. He slowed slightly, thinking that he was probably safe, and just at that moment he felt a powerful blow to his chest and fell heavily to the earth. He tried to crawl away, fearing the impact of another bullet, but had to give up the attempt. His face contorted with pain, he raised his six-gun, prepared to sell his life as dearly as possible. Gunfire still rang out but it was sporadic and after a short time it ceased altogether. His chest hurt and a dark mist threatened to envelop him. He lay back, trying to maintain his concentration, but despite his best efforts he began to lose consciousness. His pistol slipped from his hand and the last thing he remembered before the black veil finally descended was seeing two men standing over him with their guns pointing at his head.

When he came round, the guns were still there and behind them were two faces, one of which was vaguely familiar. Above their heads, stars were beginning to appear in the evening sky. Strangely, the pain in his chest had subsided. One man was watching him closely and, as Buchanan's eyes focused on him, his face twisted in an ugly grin.

'Well,' he said, addressing his companion, 'it looks like our friend has finally decided to join us.'

The other man spat. 'Not for long,' he said.

Buchanan was taking the time to gather his scattered wits and try to recall where he had seen the man's face before. Then he remembered. The face was that of the man he had shot in the hand; wasn't his name Wheeler?

'You've put us to a considerable amount of inconvenience,' Wheeler said.

'He shot Quint,' the other man muttered.

In response, Wheeler turned to him with a scowl on his countenance. 'Never mind Quint,' he hissed.

The other man didn't respond and Wheeler turned his attention back to Buchanan. He held up his hand across which a scar was burned deeply. 'See this,' he said. 'This is your doin'.'

Buchanan summoned up a grin. 'I shouldn't have been so careful,' he replied.

His words seemed to enrage Wheeler; raising his foot, he slammed it into

Buchanan's side. Buchanan winced and gasped for breath.

'Get up,' Wheeler said.

Buchanan managed to struggle to his feet, but the effort left him exhausted. Wheeler was not prepared to make allowances.

'OK,' he rapped, 'start walkin'.'

By way of encouragement, he rammed his gun into Buchanan's back. Summoning up all his reserves of strength, Buchanan began to stagger forward. After a few steps he fell to his knees and the second gunman dragged him upright.

'Keep walkin',' Wheeler grunted.

Buchanan had no option but to do as he was ordered. The going was uphill and the strain was almost too much for him, but somehow he succeeded in carrying on. His chest began to ache once more; it felt as though he had been kicked by a mule. He reached down and winced as his fingers touched a huge bruise. There was something else: the battered remnants of his Bible. Suddenly he realized what had happened. The bullet he had received had buried itself in the book. He was very lucky to still be alive. If it were not for that, the bullet would have entered his chest and killed him. Shefflin's Bible had saved him.

After what seemed an eternity he saw the grim outline of the dead tree outlined against the sky. Tethered nearby was a horse. Even in his condition, Buchanan couldn't help reflecting that it must be one of those acquired by Dugmore for the Pony Express — maybe the very one he had been meant to ride. Below them, the cabin with its adjoining stable seemed already quite far away.

'Where are you takin' me?' he said.

Wheeler's face twisted in an evil grin. 'You'll see soon enough,' he replied.

Buchanan's chest was giving him a lot of pain, but at least it was only bruising and nothing worse. He was sure that nothing had been badly damaged.

They were almost beneath the blasted tree now. Looking at it, Buchanan noticed for the first time that a rope had been thrown across the lowest branch. Suddenly a cold shiver ran down his back. So that was it. They were going to lynch him.

'Go get the horse,' Wheeler said to his fellow gunslick.

In a moment the horse was brought round and placed in position beneath the tree and after the noose was placed about his neck, Buchanan was manhandled aboard. It took some effort on the part of his assailants and they took a few moments to recover their breath. Even if he had thought of something he might do to avert his imminent fate, Buchanan was in no condition to be able to carry it out.

'You didn't think you were gonna get away with shootin' me, did you?' Wheeler snarled.

Buchanan looked down at him. 'You seem to be goin' out of your way to prove a point,' he said.

'Count yourself lucky you ain't sufferin' any worse. I'm treatin' you too light.' The horse stamped and Wheeler reached for its bridle to calm it.

'A man about to die gets to have one last request,' Buchanan said, stalling for time.

Wheeler laughed. 'Go right ahead,' he said. 'There ain't no rush. I'm enjoyin' this.'

Buchanan was trying to think, but his head felt fuzzy and the pain in his chest was bad. There was a drumming sound in his ears which seemed to grow louder by the second. Suddenly he realized that it was not in his head but was coming from outside. In the same instant, Wheeler turned and drew his six-gun as he realized that the sound was made by the drumming of hoofbeats. Frantically, Buchanan clawed at the rope around his neck as the place exploded in a cacophony of gunfire. The horse on which he was seated broke forward just as the rope came free and he felt his head jerk as he fell backwards from the saddle. He heard a blood-curdling scream from nearby and looked up to see Wheeler stagger as blood pumped from his neck. The gun in his hand fired once more and then he fell

163

backwards, landing with a heavy clump next to Buchanan. For a moment their eyes met. There was a strange, questioning look on Wheeler's face and then it was replaced by a blank nothingness as he jerked twice and then lay still. The other gunnie had his hands in the air and was shouting something at the top of his voice. The shooting stopped along with the beat of horses' hoofs. Buchanan heard footsteps running towards him and a voice calling his name. Someone came up and knelt beside him. He was confused and hurting and didn't know what was happening, but the last thing of all he would have expected to see was the face of his uncle looking down at him.

'Evan,' he breathed, 'are you OK?'

He managed to summon a wan smile. 'I think so,' he said. 'But hell and tarnation, that was a close thing.'

'Who are these two varmints?'

'One of them is the low-down coyote I shot in the hand. I don't know what they were doin' here, but they must have been out for revenge.'

Caird was looking closely at the bruising to his nephew's chest. 'Us gettin' here in the nick of time wasn't the only close thing,' he said.

'My chest sure hurts,' Buchanan replied.

'You're lucky it ain't got a big hole in it.'

Buchanan struggled to a sitting position. It was only then that he noticed Horner and Kitson.

'Get him down to the relay station,' Horner said.

'You reckon you can walk that far?' Caird asked his nephew. Buchanan nodded but grimaced as he did so. 'If you two round up the horses and bring 'em down, I'll take care of Evan.'

'What about him?' Kitson said, nodding in the direction of the remaining gunnie.

Caird looked at the man. He cut a forlorn figure as he watched them anxiously.

'Turn him loose,' Caird said.

Kitson turned to the man. 'You heard,' he snapped. 'Start walkin'.'

'What about my horse?' the man said.

'Don't push your luck,' Kitson replied.

The man hesitated but at another movement from Kitson, he turned and began to walk away.

'Keep well clear of the relay station,' Caird shouted. 'You'd better not let any of us clap eyes on you again.'

'He's gettin' off light,' Horner commented. 'If justice were served, it'd be him hangin' from that tree.'

Caird watched the man's retreating figure for another moment and then suddenly sprinted after him. The man looked round in alarm as Caird seized him by the shoulder.

'One more thing,' Caird snapped. 'What do you know about someone called Grote?' The man hesitated and Caird shook him violently.

'OK,' he said, 'just give me a moment. Look, all I know is that he was workin' for Mr Dugmore.'

'The owner of the Bar U? And the proprietor of the new Pony Express service?' The man nodded. 'Grote and a gang of gunslicks were seen leavin' the Bar U earlier today. What do you know about that?'

'Nothin'. I heard a rumour they were headin' for some spread west of here called the White Sage. Honestly, that's all I know.'

Caird glared hard at him. 'You sure about that?' he snapped.

'I got no cause to lie,' the man said.

Caird continued to hold him in an iron grip before finally releasing him. The man didn't waste any time but turned and continued to walk away. Caird watched him for a few moments and then turned to join the others.

'Come on,' he said to Buchanan. 'We'd better get you down to the cabin and see about that injury of yours.'

Late in the afternoon of the day of the inaugural run of the new Pony Express, Marshal Bedford made his way to the Marietta Eating House. The place was closed but when she saw his approach, Marietta opened the door to admit him.

'After a day like this, I reckon you could do with some strong black coffee,' she said.

'You know me too well,' he replied.

He sat at a table while she went to prepare the coffee. It would soon be dusk and the crowds had finally dispersed. There had been a few incidents when people, under the influence of too much drink, had threatened to cause trouble, but he had been quick to intervene and put a stop to it. A couple of the more persistent troublemakers were kicking their heels in the jailhouse. Down at Logan's things were remarkably quiet, and the marshal put it down to the fact that Dugmore's hardcore gunmen who tended to congregate there were out of town, riding with Grote.

His thoughts were occupied with Dugmore. The evidence against the businessman was growing. There could be little doubt that he was a dangerous rogue and he was considering whether the time might have come to do something about it and bring him in for questioning.

It didn't seem right or fair that a couple of hot-headed drunks should be spending time in the slammer while someone like Dugmore walked free. It was a question of justice. The fact that Dugmore and his enterprises, of which the new Pony Express service was the latest, contributed considerably to the prosperity of Sand Ridge was beside the point.

He was immersed in these thoughts when Marietta appeared carrying a tray on which were a pot of coffee and two cups.

'You don't mind if I join you?' she said.

'Of course not. I'll be glad of your company.'

She took a seat next to him and poured out the coffee. 'You don't take alcohol, do you?' she said.

'Nope. In my line of business, I figure it's best that way.'

'You do a good job,' she said. 'The folks of this town have a lot to thank you for.' They each took a sip of the thick black liquid.

'By Jiminy, that's good,' Bedford

commented.

'I reckon I should know by now how you like it,' she replied. He glanced at her and smiled.

'It's been a busy day,' he said. 'If you're anythin' like me, you must be feelin' pretty tired too.'

'All the celebratin' has been good for custom,' she said, 'but I have to admit I'm kinda glad days like this don't come round too often.' They were silent for a while, beginning to relax and appreciate one another's company, before Marietta spoke again.

'Miranda has done very well today,' she said. 'I would have found it very hard without her.'

'That's good,' the marshal replied. 'To be honest, I didn't think the Eastwater Hotel was the best place for her. I figure she's much better suited to workin' here.'

Marietta gave him a quizzical look. 'Why do you say that?' she said.

'I don't really know. I guess I mean she's young and untried. She couldn't do better than to have someone like you keep an eye out for her and teach her the ropes.'

Marietta seemed to consider his words. 'It's funny you should say that,' she concluded. 'Listen, do you mind if I talk to you about something?' It was Bedford's turn to look quizzical.

'I know I can trust you not to mention what I'm about to say to anyone else. You see, I promised I wouldn't say anything about it, but I can't keep it to myself and you're the only person I can speak to.'

'Is this somethin' to do with Miss Glover?' the marshal asked.

'Yes.' Marietta paused and then taking a breath, continued, 'When Miranda — Miss Glover — started working here, I noticed she was very quiet. I've known her for a while and I had a feeling something was not quite right. Well, I eventually found out what it was.' A crease had appeared in Bedford's brow as he paid close attention to what Marietta was saying.

'It wasn't easy getting her to open up, but in the end she did.'

'What happened?' Bedford prompted.

'You know who owns the Eastwater Hotel?' Marietta asked.

'Yeah, sure. Leroy Dugmore owns it, and half the rest of the town as well.'

'Well, it seems that Dugmore wasn't content just to employ Miranda as a waitress. He expected other benefits as well.'

'You mean —'

'Dugmore attempted to rape her. It was only by using her wits and putting up a struggle that she managed to escape his attentions.'

Bedford's expression was grim. 'Are you sure about this?' he asked. 'I mean, that what Miranda said happened really did happen? We both agree she's young and inexperienced. She couldn't have mistaken Dugmore's intentions?'

'She's telling the truth,' Marietta replied. 'I've told you what she said quite bluntly. I've not gone into details and I haven't said anything about how upset she was.'

'Of course,' Bedford replied. 'I apologize for raisin' the question, but it was one I had to ask.' He looked out of the window, partly to recover his composure and partly to consider his response.

'To be honest,' he said, turning back to Marietta, 'I'm not as surprised as much as I might have been. I've never liked Dugmore and I have pretty good reasons to suspect some of his activities have been outside the law. In fact, I was thinkin' about him just now before you brought over the coffee.'

'I feel the same. I haven't had much to do with the man, but he's always struck me as a weasel behind those fancy clothes and manners.'

'Thanks for tellin' me this,' Bedford said. 'Obviously, you can rely on me to keep it to myself.'

'It's a relief to be able to confide in someone else,' Marietta replied.

The marshal got to his feet. 'Thanks, too, for the coffee.' Marietta arose and accompanied him to the door, where he turned to her. 'You can take it from me that Dugmore won't get away with anythin' he's done.'

'Keep me informed,' she replied. He nodded and smiled before putting his hat back on his head.

'Get some rest,' he said.

He stepped out into the street as Marietta closed the door behind him. For a moment or two he stood breathing in the evening air. The bunting from the day's events flapped in the breeze and litter blew along the street. Lamps were being lit in the windows of the Eastwater Hotel where, even now, Dugmore was probably still celebrating his success. With a glance in that direction, Bedford stepped down from the boardwalk and began to make his way to his office. It made sense to wait a while till he could be certain that things had quieted down at the Eastwater Hotel before going across there and putting Dugmore under arrest.

When Caird and Buchanan were joined by the others back at the relay station, it soon became apparent what had happened there when the bodies of two men, who were obviously the station keeper and the stock tender, were found in the outhouse. Both had been shot in the back.

'I wish I hadn't set that varmint free after seein' this,' Caird remarked. The others felt a frustrated sense of anger.

'You were plumb lucky to come away with your life,' Kitson said to Buchanan.

'At least we can give 'em a decent burial,' Horner commented.

Buchanan looked puzzled. 'I don't understand why they did it,' he said. 'I could have shot to kill but I didn't. I don't see why Wheeler had to take it so badly.'

'I guess varmints like him ain't the same as you or me,' Kitson replied.

'Maybe not, but there was no need for them to go killin' these people.'

'They must get some kind of pleasure out of it,' Horner said.

Buchanan turned to his uncle. 'I owe you,' he said, 'but I can't stay around.'

'What do you mean?' Caird replied. 'I know we've bandaged up that wound of yours, but you're still not in any fit state. You need to rest.'

'I'm fine now,' Buchanan said.

'Besides, you don't want to be stickin' around here any longer than you need. I know you are all just itchin' to get back on the trail of Grote and his gang of gunnies.'

'What are you intendin' doin'?' Caird asked. 'I kinda figured you'd be joinin' forces with us.'

'I'd like that, but there's somethin' else I gotta do first.'

'What are you talkin' about?'

'I gotta get through with the mail.'

Caird looked hard at his nephew. 'Are you crazy?' he asked.

'What happened here doesn't affect the issue. I swore an oath: the mail first, the horse second, the rider last of all.'

'Those varmints who ambushed you were Dugmore's men. Doesn't that make a difference?'

'It might in the long run, but all I know right now is that I need to get back on that mustang and get to Indian Flat just as quick as I can.'

'Isn't what happened here a lesson to you?' Caird said. 'How do you know there ain't someone else waitin' to backshoot you further along the line?'

'That isn't likely,' Buchanan said. Caird was about to expostulate but quickly realized there was no point.

'Listen,' he said, 'once you've delivered that mail, head for the White Sage.'

'I can't do that. I have to stick around to pick up mail headin' in the other direction.'

'Back to Sand Ridge?'

'That's right. Remember, I'm an employee of the Pony Express now.'

Caird was at a loss what to say, but Buchanan didn't give him time to think it through. The mustang was ready and he climbed back into leather.

'You take care,' he said, 'and don't worry about me. One way and another, I'll be seein' you.' Lifting his hat to the others, he spurred the mustang and rode out of the yard into the night.

'Well,' Horner said, watching him go, 'I guess it ain't no use us hangin' about here. We got things to do and we need do 'em quickly if we're gonna back on the trail of Grote and his boys.'

Caird raised a weary grin. 'I haven't forgotten,' he said.

'The way I see it, Grote and his gang will be campin' for the night,' Kitson commented. 'We might not get much sleep, but once we get goin', we won't be too far behind.'

'OK,' Horner said. 'Then let's get goin'.'

Kitson was right. Up ahead, Grote and his gang of desperadoes had set up camp. Most of them had turned in for the night, but Grote was wakeful. He was keen to be on the move early. The quicker they did so, the quicker they would reach the White Sage. He sat a little apart from the others, turning things over in his mind. He had been this way once before and he wasn't entirely happy about retracing his steps. He felt that his previous efforts had not been appreciated by Dugmore. It galled him that Dugmore had not acted more decisively in the first place. It had also occurred to him that after what had happened last time, the White

Sage cowboys might be more prepared to meet any opposition. All in all, he was dissatisfied with the state of things, and was feeling more than ever that it would soon be time for him to light a shuck. He didn't like Dugmore; that was the top and bottom of it. He was sitting meditating on these things when one of the men approached him.

'I figured you should know,' he said. 'There's a rider headed this way.'

'A rider?'

'He's a long way off. There's probably nothin' in it.'

'Let me take a look.'

The man led the way to an outcrop of rock which commanded a view over the moon-drenched landscape and handed Grote a pair of field-glasses. Grote clapped them to his eyes and took a long look before putting them aside.

'Whoever it is, he's veered off and taken a different trail,' he said. He put the glasses back to his eyes. The rider was a distant dot and as he watched he disappeared from view.

'Hell,' he said as he handed the glasses back, 'it's probably one of those Pony Express riders taken a wrong turn and got lost.'

The man grinned as Grote began to walk away. He watched his back and then looked up at the sky. The stars hung low and the moon was like a silver dollar someone had thrown into the air for someone to shoot at.

7

When Caird and his companions left the Dead Tree station, the first glimmerings of dawn were in the air. Despite the night's activities and the lack of sleep, they were feeling surprisingly alert. They were aware that their quarry could not be too far ahead of them and were braced for the forthcoming encounter.

'I wonder how Buchanan is doin',' Horner said to Caird as they rode side by side.

Caird didn't reply but only grunted. He figured that the boy was out of danger as far as being bushwhacked was concerned, but he had a long ride ahead of him and the bruising to his chest was pretty bad. Well, Buchanan was on his own again now. He would just have to take his chances, the same as themselves. They all knew the odds were stacked against them. The gunslicks out-numbered them four to one. On the other hand, they were prepared and the gunnies were unaware of their presence. That had to count for something. In any event, they had gone into it with their eyes open. All that remained was to see it through.

It didn't take them long to strike Grote's trail; a troop of horsemen like the one he was riding with left an unmistakable mark, and by mid-morning they had come across the remnants of his camp. They stopped and getting down, began a cursory examination of the site. Among the detritus were a few bottles of rot-gut whiskey.

'With any luck,' Horner commented, 'they'll be feelin' the after-effects of this stuff.'

They remounted and rode on. They knew they were closing in on Grote and his gang and were on the alert for the first visible sign of them. Before much time had passed they detected a distant cloud of dust and drew to a halt.

'From now on we're gonna have to be extra careful,' Horner said. 'If we can see them, they might be able to see us.'

'The way I look at it,' Caird commented, 'it might be an advantage if we could somehow get ahead of them.'

Kitson was looking around, observing the lie of the land. To their left the terrain rose towards a low-lying range of hills.

'I got an idea,' he said. 'I know this country. My cabin is over beyond those hills. There are various small valleys and water courses leading through. If we take a cut-off I got in mind, we can do that.'

'Get ahead of 'em?'

'Yes. The trail they're riding follows the line of the hills, but we'd be drivin' right through.'

'You're sure about this?'

'Sure.'

'We might lose sight of Grote,' Horner commented.

'It wouldn't matter,' Kitson replied. 'If we follow the route I got in mind, we'd cut right across their trail in plenty of time to set somethin' up.'

Caird glanced at Horner. The oldster's face was creased in a grin. 'What are we waitin' for?' he said.

'OK,' Caird said to Kitson. 'Let's do as you say.' Without more ado they spurred their horses and headed into the hills.

Tired and weary though he was, Buchanan didn't spare either himself or his mustang but hurtled on through the night. At each of the two relay stations where he changed horses, he was half expecting to meet a similar reception as he had at Dead Tree Creek, but there were no problems apart from the fact that at the first they had given up expecting him. The station keeper and his helper were engrossed in a game of cards and there was a delay in saddling his next mount. Once astride a fresh horse, however, he wasted no further time in pressing on.

He was tired out. His chest ached and his limbs seemed to be weighted with lead. His head, however, remained clear. The night was translucent with moonshine and starlight and he had no difficulty following the trail. He dropped low over his horse as it raced on across an eerie landscape carpeted with sage and straggling greasewood. By the time he was nearing the end of his journey, he figured he couldn't be too far behind schedule. He couldn't have said why, but it was important to him to arrive on time.

The stars were beginning to fade when he finally came in sight of the home station at Indian Flat. The main building was a substantial log structure considerably larger than the others. This time the station keeper and stockman were ready and waiting as he drew his horse to a sliding halt and dropped from the saddle. He stood, drawing breath, while the *mochila* was removed and slung across the saddle of a fresh horse.

'You look like you could use some sleep,' the station keeper said.

The new Express rider quickly mounted up and in another moment he was on his way. They stood watching him for a few moments and then the station keeper turned back to Buchanan.

'What's that bandage you got swathed round your chest?' he asked.

Buchanan let out a sigh of mingled

relief and exhaustion. 'I had some trouble,' he responded.

'That's what I figured,' the station keeper said. He glanced at the stockman and then back at Buchanan.

'Come on inside,' he said. 'Make yourself at home.'

The morning sun was gaining in strength as Caird and his companions positioned themselves on a hillside overlooking the trail along which Grote and his gang must soon appear. Kitson's cut-off had saved them a lot of miles and distance and Caird had been impressed by the old mountain man's knowledge of the terrain. Their situation was a good one. They had plenty of cover and the advantage of high ground with a good view over the trail below. The element of surprise was also theirs and they could only hope that these positive aspects would serve to offset the fact that they were seriously outgunned. However, Caird was hoping there might be a way to avoid bloodshed. It was Grote they were after; maybe the gunnies could be persuaded to hand him over, especially if they had cause to believe they were facing bigger odds than was the case. They had no particular reason to stand by him. As far as Caird could make out, he wasn't exactly a popular figure. If necessary, though, they were all well prepared for gunplay. When he had taken up his position in the shelter of a rocky outcrop, he took the time to check his six-guns. The loops of his belt were filled with shells and he also wore a second belt with slugs for the Paterson. Horner and Kitson were similarly well supplied. He looked across to where they were stationed and they met his glance with a wave of the arm. Then he looked to where the trail wound its way round the outlying slopes of the hills.

It wasn't long till he heard a distant drum of hoofbeats. As they came closer they seemed to echo and rebound from the hills and it would have been hard to place from which direction the riders were coming if the trail had not been apparent. Soon the riders came into view and he looked at them through his field-glasses. Although he had come across Grote only once before, he thought he recognized him. In any case, it was fairly obvious which one was him, riding at the head of the group. He put the glasses down and glanced at the others once more. They were ready. As the riders drew closer, he took a long breath, drew one of his six-guns and fired a single shot into the air. The effect was instantaneous as the riders drew to a halt and began to look anxiously around them.

From his place of concealment behind the rock, Caird called out in a loud voice, 'That was a warnin' shot. I'd advise you not to try anything. We have you covered and we're ready to kill every last man of you if needs be. But that shouldn't be necessary. It's Grote we want, to answer charges of murder and arson. The rest of you can just ride away.'

He paused to see the effects of his harangue. It seemed to be working. The gunnies were looking about them and the expressions on their faces were ones of puzzlement and surprise. Caird thought he could detect another element too — one of fear. Some of them were looking towards the man who had been leading the group as if they expected him to do or say something, but he seemed as agitated as the rest of them. For a few moments all was confusion and Caird was about to take advantage of it when Grote's horse suddenly shot forward and began to gallop off down the trail. At the same moment there was a flash of light and the boom of a rifle and a bullet struck a rock surprisingly close to where Caird was lying. The effect was instantaneous; more shots began to ring out as the gunnies, caught by surprise as much as Caird and his companions, began to respond in the only way they knew. A melee was taking place among the riders; horses reared and mingled together in confusion as some of the gunnies dropped from their saddles and sought shelter while others tried to follow in Grote's tracks. There was no way now of avoiding bloodshed, and it didn't require a signal from Caird for Horner and Kitson to begin blazing away with their rifles.

Caird's eyes were following the rapidly disappearing Grote. It seemed like he was going to get away, in which case all their efforts would have been in vain, but suddenly Grote's horse took a tumble and Grote went flying over its head. It looked a bad fall but in a moment he was back on his feet. He grabbed his rifle from the stricken animal and scrambled for cover while the horse, recovering its feet, careered on down the trail. Pumping a bullet into his rifle barrel, Caird lined his sights on the spot where Grote had found shelter and pressed the trigger. Even as he did so, he realized it was useless. The man was out of range. Before he had time to do anything further, he had to duck as lead ricocheted around him. Any thoughts that the gunnies might have been fooled as to the numbers they were facing were gone now. Once the shooting started, they could work that out. The outlook was not good. Something needed to be done, and quickly. Caird glanced up at the slope of the hillside behind him. There was fairly good cover; perhaps they could make their way up to the place on the other side where they had left their horses. Lifting himself slightly, he signalled to the others and shouted at the top of his voice above the cacophony of the guns.

'Move upwards but stay under cover!'

Taking advantage of the protection of the rocks, he gingerly got to his knees and began to crawl away. The gunslicks' shooting had become rather wild and Caird was gaining in confidence when a slug whined dangerously close overhead and slammed into a rock, sending up a spray of shards, one of which cut into his cheek, drawing blood. Caird lay low for a few moments, trying to locate the gunman's place of concealment. Another flash indicated the likely spot and as a face briefly appeared, he opened fire. There was a scream and the face disappeared from view. At almost the same moment, he detected a sign of movement in some bushes fairly close to Horner; he pumped his rifle action and squeezed the trigger. This time there was no answering cry and he couldn't be sure whether or not he had hit his target. Horner, however, seemed to take the warning as he turned and blazed away in the same direction. These sudden outbursts of gunfire were followed by a slight lull. They were making good progress, slithering and crawling away from the main danger area. Caird gave a signal for them to curtail their fire as far as possible, hoping not to give away their exact position. In the sudden quiet, he could hear the gunslicks' voices and strained his ears to hear what they were saying. From the odd words and phrases he was able to pick up, it seemed they were questioning the wisdom of carrying on with the fight.

'Where's Grote?' he heard a voice distinctly ask, and another voice answered: 'He's taken off … further down the trail.'

'He's left us to fight his fight,' someone yelled.

'Are you boys ready to throw it in?'

He glanced behind him and saw that

some of the gunslicks had returned to their horses. A couple of them were already riding back in the direction from which they had come. Then he turned his head the other way and saw something else. Grote had emerged from cover and was making his way towards where his horse stood at a little distance. He must have known he was out of range because he was making no effort to conceal himself. The others saw him too and realized the significance of it. Casting a last look at the scene behind them, they sprinted forward till they reached their own horses and sprang into leather.

As they rode, they could see that the gunnies had now dispersed in several directions. A couple were riding after Grote, but that individual was well ahead of them and seemed to exhibit no knowledge of their presence. It wasn't at all clear, either, whether Grote was aware of Caird and his companions. They were a good way behind but they had him in their sights. He was riding hard. A grove of trees loomed up on the path ahead and he vanished from view. Caird strained his eyes, watching out for Grote to emerge back on the trail, but he didn't reappear. Reluctantly, they drew their horses to a halt.

'Where the hell has he gone?' Horner rapped.

They waited, still hoping and expecting to see him, but it was soon evident they had lost him.

'He must have left the trail and taken a different way among those trees,' Kitson remarked.

'You know the country? Can you think of anywhere he might be headed?'

'I can think of a few places, but you're forgettin' that the country is new to Grote. He probably hasn't got anythin' else in mind other than to make good his escape.'

The gunslicks who had ridden off in the same direction presently appeared back on the trail. They were riding in a desultory fashion which seemed to indicate that they were not seeking their former leader. They carried on down the trail and finally were lost to view round a bend.

'What now?' Horner asked.

'We came to get Grote and bring him to justice. Let's get down among those trees and see if we can pick up his sign.'

They wheeled their horses in the direction of the trees and rode on till eventually they arrived at the spot where Grote had disappeared. Although it was not evident at the distance from which they had seen him, there was a side-trail leading into the trees. They pushed on and after a short distance it opened out into rolling country leading back towards the hills. They were looking out for indications of Grote's passage but they couldn't find anything to go on. There were various side trails which he could have chosen and after a time they came to a halt again, uncertain whether they might have taken the wrong one.

'Seems to me we're gonna have to split up,' Kitson said.

'I don't like the idea, but I guess you're right,' Caird replied. Horner wasn't happy either, but he saw the sense of what the others were saying.

'Where do you think Grote would make for?' Caird asked. 'I mean, in the longer run.'

'Back to the Bar U, I guess,' Horner replied.

'I'm not so sure,' Kitson replied. 'After what just happened, he might not want to run into his cronies again. He might just decide to cut and run.'

'Well, I guess we haven't got much choice. Buchanan will be headin' back for town eventually. If we can't find any trace of Grote, we'll meet up back at the Dead Tree Station and then make our way to Sand Ridge.'

It wasn't much of a plan, but none of them could think of a better. With a final word of caution regarding Grote, they took off in different directions, each one of them still hopeful of catching up with their target.

Since Kitson knew the hill country best, Caird and Horner set off along side trails in opposite directions. For a while they remained in sight of each other but eventually each man was on his own. Caird carried on riding at a steady pace, still looking about him for evidence of Grote having passed that way. He was losing confidence that any of them would catch up with him when he saw, a long way up ahead, the figure of a lone rider. Instantly he tensed. It might not be his quarry. It could even be one of the other gunnies. But something told him it was Grote, and told him too that he was gaining ground and slowly catching up with him.

He rode down into a depression and then up the other side. The roan was going strong and showing no sign as yet of tiredness. He felt it still had something more to give and urged it to greater speed. He came up the opposite slope of the depression and carried on across a valley floor covered with sage and patches of mesquite with occasional clumps of trees. Because of the rolling nature of the terrain, he had lost sight of Grote and after a time he drew the horse to a halt. Tying it to a stunted bush, he took his field- glasses and climbed to a high point. The undulations of the land were stretched out before him and even with his naked eye he could see the rider. When he looked through the glasses, he could see that it was the same person who had ridden off at the commencement of the fight with the gunslicks. Satisfied as to which direction he should go, he returned to the roan, climbed into the saddle, and rode on.

He carried on until he saw, still some way ahead, a tiny creek shaded by willow and cottonwoods. His first reaction was one of relief. His horse was in need of water and he could take the opportunity to refill his canteen. He moved towards it, but then suddenly drew up. If he and his horse were in need of refreshment, then the same should apply to Grote. Wouldn't he be in exactly the same situation? He peered ahead, but he could see no sign of movement. Still, he had a premonition that Grote was there. He began to dismount but then had a change of mind. Instead of trying to creep up on Grote, he would ride hard straight for the creek. If he was right about Grote being there, it seemed Grote wasn't yet aware of Caird's presence. If he was wrong, nothing would be lost. Having made the decision, Caird drew his six-gun and then dug his spurs into the horse's flanks.

It shot forward and was quickly into its stride. Caird, lying low along the length of its back, felt the wind in his hair and flecks of foam from the horse's mouth flew backwards into his face. The trees bordering the creek came towards him with bewildering speed as the horse lengthened its stride even further and tore along the ground with its hoofs beating a loud staccato rhythm. Caird had a glimpse of another horse standing among the trees and then he had his first sight of Grote. The man had sprung to his feet and was standing in the clearing with a rifle in his hand. As Caird charged towards him, he raised it and fired. Caird felt the whine of the bullet as it flew by just over his head and he responded with his Colt Dragoon. The horse reared and then lunged as Caird fought to rein it back under control. The world was heaving crazily all about him. He tried to steady himself by making a grab for the saddle horn but he missed and felt himself falling to the ground. He landed heavily and the six-gun was knocked from his hand. He was winded but succeeded in rolling to one side as another bullet from Grote's rifle tore up dust nearby. He was acting purely from instinct as he got to his feet as rapidly as he could and zig-zagged his way to where Grote was fumbling with the Sharps. In an instant he had hurled himself on the gunslick and they both went over.

Caird was first on his feet and as Grote tried to raise the rifle, he kicked it from his hands. The movement unbalanced him and Grote's swinging leg brought him down again. They were both up again at the same moment and Grote came forward with his arms flailing and his face twisted in a grimace of rage and hatred. Caird ducked to drive a blow at Grote's midriff but it failed to register fully and

Grote responded by bringing his knee up into Caird's chin. Caird's head jerked back and he uttered a grunt of pain as blood spurted from his mouth. Grote came on again; he braced himself and met his oncoming assailant with his head. He heard a sickening crunch as Grote's nose split and spread across his face like an over-ripe piece of fruit. He staggered and fell and in an instant Caird was on top of him.

Grote reached up and raked his nails down Caird's face. The gunslinger's hands were digging and gouging but Caird had enough presence of mind to swing his fist and bring it crashing into Grote's upturned face. Blood was flowing down Caird's face, momentarily blinding him, but he continued to rain short, solid blows into Grote's face. With a desperate effort Grote arched his back and kicked out, sending Caird tumbling backwards to the ground. Grote was on his feet in an instant and when Caird looked up he found himself staring into the barrel of a derringer. The gun was inches from his forehead and with a singular clarity he registered the sunburst design with the letter P on the left side of the breech. Grote's face was livid with hate and his rancid breath came in quick gasps.

'I'm guessin' you got somethin' to do with the White Sage ranch,' he breathed.

Caird didn't answer and Grote's response was to kick him viciously in the thigh. The pain was searing but Caird saw his chance and, grabbing at Grote's leg, succeeded in pushing him backwards. As Grote struggled to regain his balance, Caird rolled over and, reaching out, found he was close to Grote's rifle which he had previously kicked from his grasp. He reached for it but it was just too far away and before he could do anything further Grote's boot descended with sickening force on his outstretched arm. Grote's face was split in an evil grin.

'Even better,' he said. He bent down and picked up the Sharps.

'They ain't gonna recognize you when they find your dead body,' Grote hissed. 'That is, if anybody ever does.'

Slowly, he raised the rifle as Caird, with

an empty sensation in the pit of his stomach, realized that his time was up and that there was nothing he could do about it. Resolutely, he refused to close his eyes. Grote's finger closed on the trigger but there was no explosion. Instead, the hammer snapped into an empty breech as the gun jammed. Grote squeezed the trigger once more and then, throwing the Sharps away, reached for the derringer he had placed back in his pocket. But he was too slow. Caird's almost miraculous moment of respite had imbued him with fresh energy and he was back on his feet, striking madly at the bewildered gunslick.

Grote staggered and reeled. The derringer was back in his hand but Caird had his wrist in an iron grip. He bent Grote's hand back but Grote began to respond and for a few moments the gun wavered and hovered one way and then another. Briefly, the gun barrel pointed in Caird's face but then it tilted away again. Suddenly there was a muffled explosion and Caird wasn't sure whether he or Grote had been shot. Then Grote's expression changed to one of surprise and blood began to gush from a corner of his mouth. His eyes looked into Caird's face and then turned upwards as if he was looking at the sky. For a few moments they remained locked together and then Grote started to slide slowly away from Caird till he lay slumped in a heap at Caird's feet. It all seemed strange and dreamlike and it took Caird some minutes to regain his sense of reality. Grote lay still and when he bent down to examine him, the only injury he could see was a neat hole in the side of Grote's temple. It was small and almost perfectly round. A trickle of blood ran from it but it didn't seem enough to have killed a man.

Marshal Bedford leaned against a stanchion and observed the street in front of him. It was a bustling scene. People passed each other along the boardwalks, going to and from the stores and emporiums; a wagon and a couple of buggies were drawn up while horsemen rode by. It was a peaceful scene and the fact that Dugmore was kicking his heels in the jailhouse awaiting the arrival of the circuit judge made no difference to it at all. That was probably because most people didn't know anything about it, but he had no doubt that when the news began to circulate, it still would make little or no impression on anyone.

He wasn't just lounging for the sake of his health, however. He was looking out for any sign of Caird and his companions. He already knew about the events that had taken place at the Dead Tree Station from Buchanan, who had returned the day before. It was more evidence against Dugmore. Buchanan had not been surprised by the news of Dugmore's arrest, although Bedford hadn't mentioned anything about what Miss Glover had told him. There was no point in getting the youngster hot around the collar. Besides, it wasn't his business to do so. If she wanted Buchanan to know, it was up to her to tell him herself. In the long run it would likely come out in court, but that was some way down the line. Buchanan knew enough about Dugmore to realize the strength of the case against him, and he had wasted no time in resigning from his role with the Pony Express. Bedford wondered idly what would be the likely outcome of that enterprise. Presumably it would fold, but it would come as no surprise. It seemed to him that the whole concept was doomed from the beginning. From what he had heard, it seemed someone had come up with the idea of stringing wire clear across the country.

He looked towards the end of Main Street and saw three riders who had just appeared. As they approached, he recognized them as Caird, Kitson and Horner. He couldn't help a slow smile from spreading across his features, although he wasn't altogether surprised to see them just then. The previous evening he had paid a visit to Logan's and observed that a couple of Dugmore's hired men were there. Since they had been members of Grote's gang, he made the assumption that Caird and his companions had probably been successful in catching up and dealing with them. When they were near he stepped out to greet them.

'Howdy,' he said. 'Good to see you back.'

'Good to see you too, Marshal,' Caird replied. They drew their horses to a halt and dismounted.

'Come inside,' the marshal said. They tied their horses to the hitch rack and followed him into the cool shade of his office.

'I figure you could use a drink,' he said. 'I don't partake myself, but I got a bottle set aside for this sort of occasion.'

Caird glanced in the direction of the Marietta Eating House. 'In that case,' he replied, 'why don't we take ourselves over there. I figure some of Marietta's coffee would hit the spot just as well.'

'Suits me,' Bedford said.

They made their way across the street and entered the eating establishment where Marietta greeted them. The marshal glanced about the room but he couldn't see Miss Glover. They took a table and soon were enjoying the slightly bitter taste of Marietta's coffee. When the marshal had taken a swallow, he looked at Caird.

'You caught up with Grote, then,' he said.

'Yup. He won't be causin' trouble any more.'

'What happened?'

Keeping his story brief, Caird outlined what had occurred. 'My intention was to bring Grote in,' he said, 'to face justice. But it didn't work out that way.'

'What did you do with the body?'

'Buried it, same as we did with those poor folk at Dead Tree Creek.'

'Sounds like you were lucky to come out of it alive yourself,' the marshal commented.

'Now Grote is out of the way, I'd like to ride out to the Bar U and have a few words with Dugmore,' Caird responded. The marshal grinned.

'You won't need to go as far as the Bar U,' he said. 'He's right across the road. I got him in the jailhouse.'

In response to the puzzled looks on

the faces of Caird and his companions, the marshal set about explaining the situation. When he had finished, Horner let out a sigh.

'That no-good critter,' he said. 'It's a pity we didn't deal with him as well as Grote.'

'I know how you feel,' the marshal said, 'but it's best to let the law take its course. That's the way it's gotta be.' There was a moment's silence before he turned back to Caird.

'What about you, boys?' he asked. 'What are you figurin' to do now?'

'I guess we'd better get on back to the White Sage,' Caird replied. 'There's a trail drive that's overdue.' He turned to Kitson. 'You'd be welcome to join us. There's a job for you with the White Sage if you want it.'

Kitson shook his head. 'I sure appreciate the offer,' he said, 'but I figure it's time I got back to my old shack in the hills. Things have been kinda hectic lately and I figure I could do with some peace and quiet.'

'I might need you back here to give evidence when Dugmore comes up for trial,' the marshal said.

'Sure,' Caird replied. 'We'll be glad to oblige.'

'You figure Buchanan will be joinin' you?'

'I'm hopin' so. There's nothing to keep him here now he's given up ridin' for the Pony Express.' The marshal grinned.

'Well,' he said, 'I wouldn't be too sure about that.' Caird gave him a quizzical look.

'Take a look out the window,' Bedford prompted.

Caird drew back the gauze curtain and they all peered out. Coming down the street was Buchanan walking side by side with Miranda Glover. It seemed as though they were making for Marietta's but they turned off just before reaching the eating house and soon became lost to view. Caird leaned back in his chair and swallowed a mouthful of coffee.

'Well,' he said, 'I guess the days when the mail came first are well and truly over.

I sure don't know what his ma is goin' to think about his doin's this time.'

We do hope that you have enjoyed reading this large print book.

Did you know that all of our titles are available for purchase?

We publish a wide range of high quality large print books including:
Romances, Mysteries, Classics
General Fiction
Non Fiction and Westerns

Special interest titles available in large print are:
The Little Oxford Dictionary
Music Book, Song Book
Hymn Book, Service Book

Also available from us courtesy of Oxford University Press:
Young Readers' Dictionary
(large print edition)
Young Readers' Thesaurus
(large print edition)

For further information or a free brochure, please contact us at:
Ulverscroft Large Print Books Ltd.,
The Green, Bradgate Road, Anstey,
Leicester, LE7 7FU, England.
Tel: (00 44) **0116 236 4325**
Fax: (00 44) **0116 234 0205**

DEATH MOUNTAIN

Dale Brandon

After the brutal murder of their employer, Matt Stone and Spider McCaw are determined to track down the culprits. Their search leads them to an outlaw hideout — in the area known as Death Mountain, because nobody attempting to pass has ever come back. The two friends must contend with not only the perilous mountain heights, but also a terrifying menace in a narrow canyon. Can they survive the treacherous journey and bring the killers to justice?

THE SECRET OF THE SILVER STAR

Amos Carr

Outlaw Vince Lange hides a deadly secret: he is really Deputy Marshal Charlie Dane, working undercover to bring down the Carlin gang. When a heavy snowstorm traps the bandits in their hideout, life becomes even more difficult for Dane when Frank Carlin sends him and another outlaw to fetch supplies — but only Dane returns, leaving three bodies and a burned-out ranch behind. Deciding to split the gang and head for the nearest town, Carlin gives Dane a terrible task to complete . . .

RANGE BOSS

Jack Edwardes

The once-prosperous Bar Circle spread has been going downhill since its former owner was found dead in a saloon girl's bed, leaving behind debt and unhappy ranch-hands who talk of quitting. Cattle have been taken by rustlers, and the new owner is struggling to defend the place. Hearing of the ranch's plight and spying the chance to make a quick buck, men are circling like coyotes, ready to kill anyone who stands in their way . . .

JEFFERSON'S SADDLE

Will DuRey

When Charlie Jefferson arrives in the Texas town of Mortimer, left for dead after a brutal ambush and robbery, he is intent on finding the man who did this to him. But he is unwittingly drawn into a plot involving the town council. For, en route to Mortimer from the wasteland where he was left to perish, Jefferson stumbled across a dying Texas Ranger. And by showing mercy to the man, he may have sealed his own fate . . .

RECKONING AT EL DORADO

Scott Connor

When Buster McCloud is accused of killing Aaron Knight and Salvadora Somoza, Marshal Lincoln Hawk wastes no time in arresting him. McCloud confesses to killing Aaron, but swears he never hurt Somoza. Hawk's investigation concludes that she is still alive — and she's not the only woman to have gone missing recently. With all the evidence pointing to ruthless gold prospector Domingo Villaruel, Lincoln must travel into the very heart of the man's empire to uncover the truth.

DEAD MEN DON'T BLEED

Walter L. Bryant

Brothers Ray and Buck Norris quit the Rebel army in 1863 and go their separate ways. Whilst Ray seeks vengeance on those who killed their parents, Buck has had enough of killing, and drifts for eleven years until he reaches Rymansville. There, he immediately runs into trouble. After going to the rescue of a young woman, he is arrested by a marshal who mistakes him for Ray — now a wanted fugitive . . .